Minuk ASHES *in the* PATHWAY

GIRLS *of* MANY LANDS

England ➤ 1592
Isabel: Taking Wing by Annie Dalton

France ➤ 1711
Cécile: Gates of Gold by Mary Casanova

China ➤ 1857
Spring Pearl: The Last Flower by Laurence Yep

Yup'ik Alaska ➤ 1890
Minuk: Ashes in the Pathway by Kirkpatrick Hill

India ➤ 1939
Neela: Victory Song by Chitra Banerjee Divakaruni

Minuk ASHES *in the* PATHWAY

by Kirkpatrick Hill

Visit our Web site at **americangirl.com**

Printed in China.
02 03 04 05 06 07 08 C&C 10 9 8 7 6 5 4 3 2 1

Girls of Many Lands™, Minuk™, and American Girl®
are trademarks of Pleasant Company.

PERMISSIONS & PICTURE CREDITS
The following individuals and organizations have generously given
permission to reprint illustrations contained in "Then and Now":
p. 187—Kuskokwim landscape, © Chlaus Lötscher; pp. 188–189—
Yup'ik girls, 1884, A. Hartmann, Moravian Archives, Bethlehem,
PA (detail); jacket and trousers, 1897, McCord Museum of Canadian
History, Montreal (M5835.1-2); pp. 190–191—fish-skin parka, © Peter
Harholdt/CORBIS; needle case with wooden tail and head, NMNH
37492, collected by E. Nelson at Ukagamut, and ivory needle case
with line and dot decoration, NMNH 38128, collected by E. Nelson
on the Lower Yukon, both courtesy of the Smithsonian National
Museum of Natural History; mother and baby and Russian Orthodox
cathedral, © Michael Maslan Historic Photographs/CORBIS;
pp. 192–193—native schoolgirls, Jesuit Oregon Province Archives,
Gonzaga University, Spokane, WA (104.12); Yup'ik girls today,
© Clark J. Mishler, c/o Mira.

Illustration by Patrick Faricy

Cataloging-in-Publication Data
available from the Library of Congress

This book is fondly dedicated to three Alaskan women:
Sylvia Olson Boullion, my friend of almost 60 years,
Ruth Olson, her mother,
and the late Pat Oakes, who loved Alaskan history.

Acknowledgments:
A book like this couldn't have been written without the
work of the explorers, travelers, and anthropologists who
carefully observed, asked questions, and wrote about what
they saw. They saved what might have been lost forever, so
that we in the 21st century can understand a little of what
it was like to be a Yup'ik girl more than 100 years ago.

Explorers Lt. Lavrentiy Zagoskin and Edward W. Nelson,
Moravian missionaries John and Edith Kilbuck and
Herman and Ella Romig, and the Russian priest at
Ikogmiut, Iakov Netsvetov, wrote about Yup'ik culture
during the 1800s. More recent writers include, among
others, Wendell H. Oswalt, Ann Fienup-Riordan, James
W. VanStone, and Dorothy Jean Ray. We are in their debt.

Finally, a special thanks to Wendell H. Oswalt, who
so kindly took the time to critique this manuscript.

Contents

Prologue

When we were little girls, we were very carefully taught what our responsibilities as Yup'ik women would be when we were grown and had families of our own.

Sometimes when we girls brought food to the men's house and were waiting for them to finish eating so we could take the dishes away, one of the old men would put a stick across the doorway. That was the signal that we were going to be taught and that no one could get up and leave.

We girls would sit on the floor, our legs stretched out, our heads lowered and our eyes down, and we would listen carefully when the old men told us about the behavior of good women.

We would be responsible for the food in our family. We had to prepare all the food that the men brought back, and gather berries and roots and see that they were stored properly. We must eat very little ourselves, and never, never could a woman eat by herself, save the best pieces for herself, or take food at any time but meals. And during the hungry times, a good woman had to feed her family before herself.

It was a woman's job not only to see that her family had enough good food; it was her job as well to see that they had good clothes that were beautifully sewn and well mended. To do that, she had to carefully tend to every skin or fur that her husband brought home.

She had to get up early, as soon as she awoke, and she must not sleep during the day, even if she was tired. Above all, she must be very careful not to spoil the men's luck by breaking any of the rules of women's behavior.

A good, modest woman who kept her family well clothed and well fed would be praised in the men's house, and her children would take good care of her when she was old and couldn't work anymore.

I would listen with my eyes on the floor, my heart nearly jumping out of my chest.

I would be a good woman. I would sew so beautifully that people would take notice of my husband and children and would praise my craftsmanship. I would take such good care of our food that I would be praised in the men's house, and there would never be too much food for me to preserve, so my husband would never have to take another wife to do any of the work.

I would be modest always and would follow all the rules for women very carefully so that no one would find fault with me.

I could hardly wait to grow up and become a woman.

But I didn't know then that being a good woman might mean something entirely different to women in other places, and that it might even mean something different to me when I grew up.

1 *Spring 1890*

We were all away at spring camp when the white people came, so they were a very big surprise to us when we got back to the village.

We children were nearly crazy with excitement. Everything they had, everything they wore, and everything they ate amazed us. And the grown-ups were just as wide-eyed as we were.

I wonder what our faces looked like the first time Panruk and I saw white people's underwear, sat on chairs, and looked through window glass. I wonder how big our eyes were!

We went to spring camp every year to fish and

hunt ground squirrels and muskrats. We needed the furs to make warm, warm parkas to wear, but, most important, we needed the extra squirrel and muskrat skins to trade for seal oil from the people at the mouth of the river. We needed at least six hundred skins, so we usually stayed at camp for six weeks.

After the animals were snared, they had to be skinned and stretched, so we were all busy from morning to night. Even my little brother Maklak worked hard.

There were thirteen of us in our family. There was Mamma, Auntie Kakgar, and Auntie Nunagak, who were Grandma and Grandpa's daughters, and there was Auntie Naya, their daughter-in-law. Auntie Kakgar was Panruk's mother. Auntie Kakgar's husband had drowned long ago. Auntie Naya was a widow, too. She had been married to Grandma and Grandpa's son, but he died before I was born. Auntie Nunagak and Uncle Aparuk had one son, Taulan.

My mother and father had one daughter, me—Minuk—and two sons. Iraluq was older than me and Maklak wasn't five yet.

In our family, all the women were good. Mamma was always patient and gentle, and never cross. Panruk's mother and our other aunties were the same.

I was not like Panruk, who was as sweet and obedient as our mothers and aunts. I wanted too often to know things—why and how and "what if." Whenever the old men spoke to us and cautioned us about modesty, I told myself that I must guard myself more carefully, so that I would do better. I was like Grandma, who had opinions. She sometimes even told the men what she thought. But she was old, and old women, because they were wiser, could say things that younger ones couldn't.

In Yup'ik villages, the men didn't live with the women. They lived all together in their own big house, the men's house. But when we went away to spring camp, the whole family lived together in one house, all thirteen of us. That was hard to get used to, because when we women lived alone, we were easier in our ways. The rules about men's tools and clothing and food were so easy to break that we were a little nervous with men living in our house—especially my father.

My father was very strict, and he never broke the rules. If anyone else broke a rule or acted frivolously, my father would be stern. He was respected in the men's house for that. He didn't have much use for talk with women, not like Grandpa, who spent a lot of time with the women in our family.

Maklak was not like our father at all. He was so merry-hearted that Grandpa used to laugh and say, "I can tell you weren't meant to be a shaman!" He said that because people always watched the serious boys to see if they looked as if they might become shamans. They never watched the laughing ones like Maklak.

I think my father was disappointed that Maklak was so happy-go-lucky. Our brother Iraluq and our cousin Taulan were not quiet or solemn either, and sometimes they broke the rules, too—but just the little ones. I think my father wished that his family was more serious, more like our Uncle Aparuk, Taulan's father. He was very quiet and hardly said anything at all. I never knew what Uncle Aparuk was thinking.

We had good luck at spring camp, and soon the cache, which we used for storage, was full of dried fish, ground squirrel and muskrat skins, and some bird skins. Although it was nice at camp, we had all become lonesome for the other people in our village. So, when the snow on the hills was gone, we were happy because it was time to put everything into our big boat and go back to the Kuskokwim River.

Getting home took us five days. It took longer going home by water than it had taken us to get to camp by dogsled, when we traveled cross-country on the hard crust of the snow.

We knew our village was near before we could

see it. We smelled wood smoke and heard children
laughing and dogs barking. Then we came around
the bend in the river, and there it was.

Most of the others had returned from their camps
before us. There were boats on the riverbank, and
Uliggaq's mother was busily going from house to
house, probably looking for her little boy. Two men
sat on top of the men's house, smoking their pipes,
and small children squatted in the mud, playing.

Maklak forgot himself and began to stand up
in the boat, he was so excited to see the children.
Grandma grabbed the edge of his parka and snapped,
"Agu! Don't!"

Maklak leaned far over the side of the boat and
yelled to the children as we turned into the bank,
"We're here! We're here!"

The children stumbled over each other in their
rush down to the riverbank to meet us and tell us what
had happened while everyone in the village had been
away at spring camp. They were all so excited that we
could hardly understand what they were saying.

Kass'aqs, white people, had built a house in our

village. They had rafted the logs down from Kolmakov as soon as the ice had moved off the river and had put up a house fast, in just a few weeks. Most of the workers had already left, but a man, his wife, and their little boy were staying in the house. They were missionaries and they were going to stay with us in our village. They'd lived for a while downriver, near where the Kuskokwim joins the ocean, so they could speak Yup'ik.

I looked at my uncle and my father and grandfather to see what they thought of this news, and although they looked up from the boat quickly to see if they could see the missionaries' house, they didn't say anything. But I saw that my father's jaw had become hard, the way it did when he wasn't pleased.

Panruk and I wanted to go see the log house right away, but of course we had to help unload the boat and get our house settled again. We quickly carried the wooden bowls and water buckets to the house, and then ran back to the boat for another load. Grandma gave us each a clay cooking pot wrapped in grass mats, and reminded us to be very careful. It was very hard not to run, we wanted so much to be finished unloading the boat! Some of the children came with us up to our house and back again, chattering all the way about the missionaries and their house and their son.

We knew about missionaries because when the Russians first came to Alaska, when Grandpa was a little boy, they had sent priests to baptize the people along the Kuskokwim River. Some of the older people had been baptized and had Russian names. Grandma had a silver cross she kept in her sewing kit, and a little picture of a lady with a circle around her head. Grandma had been given a Russian name, too, but she'd forgotten it long ago, she said.

After the Russians sold Alaska to the United States there weren't many priests left, and no priest had visited our village since I was very small. But as small as I had been then, I remembered that priest because he was so very tall and thin, and because he wore a long black robe.

I had never seen a log house built in the Russian style, though most of the grown-ups had seen them.

The Russians long ago had built a fort and trading post upriver from us at Kolmakov, and there were log houses at the mouth of the river as well. We sometimes saw Russian or half-Russian men when they came up the river to trade, and the Americans who came after them, but we'd never seen a kass'aq woman or kass'aq child.

2 Butterflies

After we had brought everything from the boat to our house, Panruk and Maklak and I went with the other children to see the new log house.

It was at the end of the village, tall and square and strong looking. It was built right on the ground, not partly buried, like our houses, and it wasn't rounded like a beaver house, the way our houses were. The roof came to a point, as if you were putting the fingertips of your two hands together.

It was made of just bare wood, its spruce logs laid sideways, and it had sod only on the roof, not covering the logs, like on our houses. There was no little passageway to get into the house, just a tall wooden door right in the front. On each side of the door were windows covered with something shiny, and on the top of the house, coming through the sod roof, was a black tube puffing smoke.

We stood far off and stared at this house for a while, and then we warily skirted around it to see what the back looked like. A very thin, tall little house with a door stood behind the big house, back by the trees, and there was a cache on tall poles, just like the ones we had to store dried fish and furs, and to hang our sleds on.

The strangest thing of all was on a line that stretched from the house to a spruce tree. The line was a rope made of something white, not walrus thongs or seal-hide cords, and on that rope was hanging a pair of blue cloth pants and a sort of pink butterfly. The butterfly thing had lacings in the middle of it instead of a body, and strings hanging down on the outside of the wing parts. It turned and twisted in the wind until the strings were all tangled.

None of the children knew what it was.

I frowned and tried to think of what it could be, but before I could imagine anything, a woman's face appeared in the back window. She smiled and waved to us. The other children gave a squeal and scampered away as fast as hares. Panruk wanted to run, too, but I held fast onto her parka. I wanted to know what that thing was.

I had been scolded many times for being too bold for a girl, and many, many times for asking too many questions. I was glad none of the grown-ups was there to see me now, for I could tell that I was full of questions and wasn't going to be able to stop them from coming out.

The face disappeared from the window, and in a second a white woman came around the corner of the house. She asked us in Yup'ik to come inside. Everything about her was so strange that I'm afraid we just stared at her. "I am Mrs. Hoff," she said. "Are you sisters?"

"No," I said. "Panruk is my aunt's daughter." I knew Panruk would not be able to speak for herself. She was very shy, except when she and I were alone together.

"And how much older are you than your cousin?" Mrs. Hoff asked me.

I laughed. "Everyone thinks I'm older," I said.

"That's because Panruk is short like her father was, and I am tall like my father. But I was born when Panruk started to walk, I think twelve summers ago."

Mrs. Hoff led us into the house. Panruk took my hand, and we both stood inside the door and looked around. It was much bigger than the house we lived in, but filled with so many things that it seemed crowded. There were chairs and tables and a big metal box, which I knew was a stove for cooking because my father had told us about the one he'd seen at the trading post upriver. Cloth hung around the windows, and there were shelves filled with tin cans and boxes that had pictures on them. The floor was made of wooden planks, just like the floor in the men's house, and there was a big thick cloth on the floor.

I could tell that Mrs. Hoff was not very old, because her hair was not yet white, and her teeth were very good and long, not worn down. She had braids, like we did, but they were brown and shiny and fastened around and on top of her head, so they didn't move.

She wasn't wearing a parka, and it was no wonder, because the house was so hot that Panruk had little beads of sweat on her upper lip, and I'll bet I did, too. Instead, Mrs. Hoff wore a pretty cloth dress with pink flowers on it, and on her feet were little black boots with lots of buttons on them. She didn't have any tattoo lines on her chin or any nose beads, but there were beads hanging from her ears.

Her eyes were blue, the same color as blueberries before they become ripe. We had seen blue eyes before—on Russian traders and on some of the half-Russian children from upriver—but still eyes that color made us feel funny.

"Sit down," she said, and pointed to the chairs around the long table near the stove. We had never sat on chairs before. Panruk was looking uncertain, so I sat down to show her that she shouldn't be afraid. But I sat so close to the front edge that the chair tipped forward, and the chair and I fell down.

"Oh, dear," said Mrs. Hoff. "Are you all right?"

Panruk started to laugh and covered her mouth quickly with her hand. I could see that it was necessary to sit far back on the chair to keep it balanced. After I did it right, Panruk sat down, too.

Then Mrs. Hoff put two red tin mugs on the table and poured some tea into them from a little pot on the stove. She put a bowl of sugar on the table and two metal spoons. We had never seen spoons that weren't carved from wood. Panruk and I were happy to put sugar into our tea. We didn't get sugar very often, but we knew how good it tasted. The mugs were so hot from the tea that we couldn't pick them up, so we put our mouths down to the mugs and slurped loudly to be polite. Mrs. Hoff gave us a look.

She spoke Yup'ik a little strangely, and some words were hard to understand, but we could always tell what she meant.

"Will you stay here for the whole summer?" I asked.

"Oh, yes, the whole summer and winter, too," she said. "I expect we'll be here for many, many years."

I was too curious to be polite, so I asked, "Mrs. Hoff, what is that thing out there, trying to fly away from the rope?"

Mrs. Hoff blinked at me. She didn't understand until I pointed out the window where we could see it jerking on the rope, the strings flying. Mrs. Hoff laughed and pressed her fingers against her cheek.

"Goodness," she said, "that's my corset."

We looked at her, waiting for her to explain. She made a wrapping motion with her hands around her middle to show us where it would go, but we still didn't know what the thing was.

"Look, I'll show you," she said. She went to a box in the other room and she took out one of the butterflies, a yellow one this time. It had hard sticks sewn inside the cloth. That was whalebone, she said. She wrapped it around her middle, over her dress and showed us how it must be laced up in the front. It must be pulled very tight, she told us. Sometimes she had to have help to get it pulled tight enough.

"What's it for?" I asked.

She looked startled, as if she thought she'd made it plain what it was for by showing us where it went.

"Well, it's to make your waist small," she said. Her waist was very small. I put my hand out to touch her waist, and instead of soft flesh under her dress there was a hard shell. That was the corset.

I could hardly believe such a thing. Imagine it

rubbing against your skin! Imagine those hard whalebone sticks digging into your stomach and chest!

"We don't wear anything under our clothes," said Panruk suddenly.

Mrs. Hoff made her mouth pinch together a little. "I know," she said.

"Why do you want your waist to be small?" I asked.

Mrs. Hoff fluttered her fingers and laughed a little. "Oh, it's just the style, you know. The way they do things where I come from."

"Does your husband wear a corset?" I asked.

Mrs. Hoff looked shocked. "Oh, no. Men never wear corsets," she said.

I thought to myself that it was unfair to make the women wear those tight corsets and let the men go free.

Mrs. Hoff looked as though she didn't want to talk about corsets anymore, so I got up and touched the shiny clear stuff in the windows. It was covered with a little mist from the teakettle. The clear stuff was hard and cold, and my hand left a pattern in the mist.

"That's window glass," she said. "It was very hard to get it here in one piece all the way up the

Kuskokwim River. It's easily broken."

She picked up a cloth and wiped the mist and my handprint away, and you could see very clearly through the glass, just as if it weren't there.

"We don't put windows in the sides of houses, only on the top," I said. "And we use seal intestines to make a window."

"I know," she said.

"Bear intestines are better, because they let in more light, and because they don't tear so easily," I said. "Maybe if this glass gets broken, you can get some bear intestines."

"I'll pray that won't happen," said Mrs. Hoff.

Then a little kass'aq boy wearing cloth pants and Eskimo boots and a store shirt came into the room. He was younger than I was, but I couldn't tell how much younger. He didn't have blue eyes; his were brown, the same color as marten fur.

Panruk and I were shocked to see him reach up to one of the shelves and take a cracker for himself from one of the boxes. It embarrassed us so much that we lowered our eyes to the floor so we wouldn't see Mrs. Hoff's shame. In the Yup'ik way, no one could ever take food without asking the mother, for she was responsible for the food and must see that there was enough for everyone.

But Mrs. Hoff was not embarrassed and didn't even seem to notice the bad behavior of her son. She spoke to her son in Yup'ik. "This is Panruk, and this is her younger cousin. This is David, my son," she said to us.

David put the cracker in his other hand and then shook hands with us very seriously and greeted us in Yup'ik. He spoke our language perfectly, better than Mrs. Hoff.

"Do you have any brothers?" he asked.

"Yes," I said. "One is not in the men's house yet, and we have two older brothers."

I could see that David was just like us. He wanted some children to play with, just as we did. I wondered if kass'aq boys liked to play the same games that Yup'ik boys played.

Mrs. Hoff opened one of the doors in the big stove and put two sticks of wood inside. We'd never seen fire inside a box like that. It looked like a very good idea to me. Our mothers cooked in the passageway of our house, which was very narrow, so it was easy to fall into the fire and burn yourself, or to have sparks make smudges on the edge of your parka.

The smoke went from Mrs. Hoff's stove up into the pipe, so there wasn't any smoke in the room. I would have been happy to have a stove with a pipe, because the smoke from our fire often made me choke so that I had to go outdoors to breathe properly.

Mrs. Hoff had some pans covered with a white cloth sitting on the table by the stove. She took the cloth off the pans and lightly touched the top of the stuff inside them with her finger.

"Ready to bake," she said. She opened the other door in the stove and put the pans inside on a little shelf.

"There. The bread will be ready in half an hour," she said.

"We don't eat bread," I said.

"Yes, I know," said Mrs. Hoff.

Panruk and I ran all the way home, afraid we'd been gone too long and would get a scolding for not tending to our chores.

When we got to our house, we saw that Mamma and the aunts had covered the floor with dry grass and spread the grass mats over that. They'd covered the sleeping benches with our caribou skins and had aired out the rabbit-skin and muskrat-skin blankets, so that everything was very tidy inside the house again.

We told them about what we'd seen at the new house. They all stopped working for a minute and listened to us. Auntie Naya had seen glass once long ago when she went to the Russian store at Kolmakov, when she was a little girl. She'd seen chairs there, too. When Grandma had gone to Russian Mission, the priest there had given them some of the white man's bread, which was soft, not like the crackers the men sometimes brought back from the trading post. But none of them had ever heard about corsets. They couldn't imagine wearing anything like that.

Grandma shook her head. *"Assiipaa,"* she said, under her breath. "How awful."

3 The Village

In other years, the first thing Panruk and I did after we got back to the village from spring camp was to get our dolls out and repair their clothes. But Panruk and I were so excited about the missionaries that we'd almost forgotten about our dolls.

So after we told Mamma and Grandma and the aunts about our visit with the Hoffs, we took our dolls out of the little fish-skin bags where they'd spent the fall and the winter. We were so happy to see them again. They were like little, dear friends we'd not seen for a long time. Even Mamma and Grandma and the aunts came out into the spring sun to touch our dolls and look at their clothes, as if they'd missed them, too. I thought that sometimes it must be hard to be grown-up and not be able to play.

Our grandfather had carved both of our dolls from driftwood. Mine had tiny lines for tattoos on the chin and little black eyes and a straight mouth. I loved her serious little face. You could tell she was a good woman.

We weren't allowed to play with our dolls in the winter. But in the spring, after the geese had returned, we could. People believed that if girls played with their dolls before spring came, the weather would see and would punish them. Then winter would come again before spring had even begun.

We took our responsibility for the weather very seriously.

Our dolls not only had lovely faces, they had wonderful clothes. Mamma and the aunts had helped us sew tiny boots and mittens and caribou pants and beautiful little parkas. The year before I had made a *qaspeq*, a parka cover, for my doll from a little bit of red calico cloth. I was very proud of that qaspeq. Panruk could sew much better than I, and she'd made a little fish-skin parka for her doll. I wasn't good enough to sew fish skin yet, which was so delicate that it tore easily. But sometimes Panruk let me put her fish-skin parka on my doll, and I let her use my qaspeq for her doll.

Because Maklak was a boy, he couldn't play with dolls, but he liked to sit near us and play with the little sled and dogs that our uncle had carved for him. Sometimes we pretended that his dog team was taking our little women to a big festival in another village, and Maklak was the driver.

Grandma had made us tiny dishes of clay and little vole-skin blankets and rabbit-fur robes, and Panruk and I had made small grass mats for our dolls' houses. Everything we had for our dolls was so little and perfect, their world became real to us. It was so real that while we played, we almost forgot about the village around us.

In our village there were five women's houses and one men's house. A women's house was called an *ena*. Each house was built partly underground. The houses looked like beaver houses, with the wood framework covered with grass and then sod.

A small, low passageway led into our house, and it

was in that passageway that we cooked. One short step up led to the big room, which was higher so that the cold couldn't come into it from the passageway. In summer, we used another entrance on the side of the house. There was a firepit in the middle of the big room, and above the firepit was the seal-gut window I had told Mrs. Hoff about. We pulled it aside to let the smoke out when we lit a fire to heat the big room.

We had a seal-oil lamp made of clay. When we needed light, we set fire to a piece of oil-soaked moss in the lamp.

Our house was not very big because there weren't too many of us. Uliggaq's house had ten women and children and Cakayak's house had fifteen, so both their houses were bigger than ours.

The men's house was called the *qasgiq*. It was much bigger than the women's houses. It had to be big, because it held all the village men, and it was where the men would stay when people came from other villages. Sometimes everyone from two villages— men and women and children—crowded into the men's house for festivals and ceremonies. There were three tiers of wide benches all around the inside of the men's house.

We were very proud of our men's house, because it was the biggest one along the whole Kuskokwim River, and it had the widest benches. The benches were so old, they had been cut with a stone ax. They had been brought long ago, before even Grandpa was born, from a men's house along the Yukon River. Our men had defeated that village in a war, so they brought the benches home to remember their victory. Our men danced that story at every big festival in the men's house, and their war cries at the end of the dance were so fierce and terrible that all of us children hid our faces.

Each man had his own place in the house, according to his age. The oldest men were nearest the door, and the youngest often slept under the benches.

There was a wooden floor in the qasgiq, even over the firepit. When the men wanted a fire, they took the boards off, but when there was a dance in the men's house, they put the floorboards back. Our feet made a good drumming sound on the wooden floor over the firepit.

In the men's house, the men made sleds and carved wooden trays and bowls and boat paddles. They made snowshoes and tools and weapons, and tanned the big skins the women couldn't handle. The men of our family lived there with all the other men. Maklak would go to live there next year, and he could hardly wait. I knew that we would miss him at home—even though he was a terrible nuisance sometimes.

The women cooked for the men in their enas and took the food to the men's house in wooden trays and bowls. Panruk and I usually did this because Mamma and the aunts were always busy. Then we sat on the floor in front of the benches, with our heads down, and waited until our men finished so that we could take the bowls away.

If we looked really quickly when we walked into the men's house, we could sometimes see what everyone was doing, but that was the only chance we got. We had to keep our eyes down at all times and could not look at any of the men or boys. I wanted so much to look out of the corners of my eyes that I was afraid someday I'd do it and disgrace myself.

Every day the men made a sweat bath in the qasgiq. First they made a fire in the firepit. They took off the smoke-hole cover so the sparks that flew up would not damage it. The fire always made a lot of thick smoke, so the men would go outside until that was gone and then put the smoke-hole cover back on. Then they went back into the qasgiq and took off their clothes. Each one had a little bundle of spruce shavings to bite on because the air was so hot and dry, it would singe their lungs if they didn't filter it. Sweat poured down the men's bodies, and their skin turned bright pink. They always competed to see who could stand the greatest heat. When they were nearly roasted, they ran outside and had someone pour cold water over their heads—or sometimes they jumped in the river.

There were a lot of things the boys got to do that the girls couldn't, and a lot of those things I was sorry about. But not the sweat bath. I never wanted to bake myself every day like that. I was glad I wasn't born a boy.

The night after Panruk and I had been in the new
people's house, Iraluq and Taulan came to our ena to
visit us, as they often did at night, and they told us
what had happened in the qasgiq that day.

Because everyone was back from spring camp,
Mr. Hoff, the missionary, had gone for the first time to
the men's house to speak to them. Some of the young
men had made noise while he spoke, pretending to be
asleep and snoring, or they sang quietly to themselves.
When my brother told us this, my cousin Taulan
looked down at his feet and smiled his full-of-mischief
smile. I wondered if he and my brother had been some
of the young men who were rude, but I didn't ask.

Some of the men didn't think the missionary should
be there, and they thought what he said was foolish.

Iraluq said Mr. Hoff's religion had a god who was the
boss of everything and who loved everyone. Mr. Hoff
told the men that the Yup'ik people were heathens.
Heathens were people, Iraluq said, who didn't believe
what Mr. Hoff believed and didn't live the same way.
Heathens couldn't go to heaven, which Mr. Hoff said
was a wonderful place to go when you were dead. If

you didn't go to heaven, you had to go to hell. Hell was a place where people were roasted in a fire that lasted forever.

I sucked in my breath when Taulan said this. I'd never heard of such a horrible thing. I looked hard at Taulan to see if he was joking, but he wasn't.

Taulan said that Mr. Hoff said that he had come to teach us about his religion so that we would not be heathens anymore and would not have to go to hell. The men had interrupted Mr. Hoff and asked him questions about what he had said, and had smiled at his answers. They said they already had a good place to go after they died, so why did they need Mr. Hoff's heaven? They said if there was a good god in charge of the world, then why did bad things happen? They asked him why, if he was a man, he lived with women and children. Only the medicine man lived with his wife. Was he a medicine man, then?

After Mr. Hoff left, the old men had talked to the other men and told them that they must be courteous to the missionary. He should be treated politely, in the Yup'ik way. They didn't have to believe what he said or follow his rules, but they had to be polite to him.

Already, the old men said, Mr. Hoff had proved that he was a hardworking man, and that he was willing to help others. He had learned their language, and if his ways were strange, they were to remember that Yup'ik ways were strange to Mr. Hoff as well.

After my brother told us all this, I told them about what Panruk and I had seen in the log house. When I told them about Mrs. Hoff's corsets, my brother and cousin laughed so hard that Grandma had to frown them quiet.

4 Mr. Hoff

It wasn't long before the other children lost their fear of the Hoffs. Many of us visited them every few days when we had time.

First, Mrs. Hoff had to teach us that it was very rude where she came from to just walk into a house. If we wanted to visit, we had to knock on the door with our knuckles, and then wait until she answered the door and asked us to come in.

We liked it when Mr. Hoff was there, too. He was a very kind man, with brown eyes and a gentle smile. If he was in the house, he would go to a tin on the shelf and get a hard piece of boiled sugar for us. There was nothing we liked better than that boiled sugar.

Sometimes Mrs. Hoff answered the door with her hair coming out of its braids and her face red, and said she was too busy to have visitors. Mr. and Mrs. Hoff were very busy because they wanted to start a school after the Berry Festival at the end of summer.

They had built a school downriver in Bethel, and two of their students had been sent far away, to a school near Mr. Hoff's home in Maryland in America. Some of the other boys who had done well in school were now church helpers, and Mr. Hoff had sent them to live in other Yup'ik villages to teach them about Mr. Hoff's religion. He did this because he said he couldn't be everywhere at once, and because it seemed that he'd no sooner left a village than everyone went back to their old way of doing things. He needed helpers to keep an eye on things and to be sure that no one broke the church rules. The boys at our school would be trained as helpers, too.

"Can't girls be helpers?" I asked Mr. Hoff.

"Women are not allowed to speak in the church. It says so in the Bible," he said.

It was the same with us. Women could not speak out in the men's house, either, so I wasn't surprised.

All summer, boats came from the mission in Bethel

with boxes of things for the school. We wanted to look at everything that came, but the Hoffs didn't even unpack the boxes. They just stacked them in their storage room. They said they'd take everything out when the new schoolroom was built.

As hard as they worked, on one day of the week the Hoffs didn't work at all. They put on clean clothes and spent most of the day just sitting. Those days, David looked out the window and waved at us. I knew he wanted to be outside, and I felt sorry for him.

That was a rule Mr. Hoff wanted the people of the village to have as well. When we became members of his church, we would have to rest one day, too, because it said so in the Bible. Mr. Hoff said the Bible was their rulebook.

People were polite to Mr. Hoff about that rule, because the old men had said we must be polite, but it bothered us to see the Hoffs sitting for a whole day. In the Yup'ik way, we worked very hard, and the only time we took a day off was in the winter, not in the summer when there was so much work to do.

We children liked to look at everything in the Hoffs' house. We always went first to look in the mirror, though, because we'd never seen ourselves in a mirror before. I think we almost expected that our faces would change from the last time we'd looked. The boys made all sorts of faces into the mirror, mostly trying to look fierce. I think they were surprised that they looked so round-faced and young in that mirror. I know that I was surprised that I looked like such a baby, my face round and stretched tight across my cheekbones.

After I got tired of looking at my face, I stood on a chair so that I could see my feet, too. My boots looked different in the mirror than when I looked down on them from the top.

After the mirror, my favorite thing was looking at the cans that were on the shelves. The pictures on the outsides of the cans showed what was inside, and there was also writing that told what the food was called. I'd never seen writing before.

"What are those marks?" I had asked Mr. Hoff.

"That's writing," he said. "When you say a word, you can put the word on paper with those marks. And then you can look at the marks and say the word back again. And that's called reading." He said *writing* and *reading* in English because there was no Yup'ik word for either one.

I must have looked puzzled, because Mr. Hoff went into another room and came back with a book, which he handed to me. It was the first time I'd ever seen a book, so I smelled it, which made Mr. Hoff laugh. But it smelled delicious, that book—sweet, like boiled sugar.

Mr. Hoff ran his finger over a line of marks and then told me what the marks said. "The marks are in the English language," he said, "but I'm saying the words in Yup'ik so that you can understand."

"Why are there four marks for just one word?" I asked.

Mr. Hoff looked pleased that I'd asked. "Each mark makes a sound, and when you put the sounds together, it makes a word."

It seemed like a wonderful idea to me, and yet so simple. I wondered why no one had thought of it before.

I stared hard at the marks on the cans, the way we'd been taught to concentrate, and the next day I made those marks in the mud by the fish racks. CORN. PEAS.

"I'm writing," I said to Panruk. I knew what each word meant because of the pictures on the cans, so I told her that corn was little yellow berries, and peas were little green berries. "And now I'm reading," I said.

Sometimes when we came to visit, Mrs. Hoff gave us magazines to look at. Panruk and I would look at one together, sitting on the floor with our backs to the wall, our legs stretched out. She and I would turn each page, carefully, whispering with awe at what we saw there.

There were tall houses, one house stacked on top of another, it looked like, and all the people were dressed like Mr. and Mrs. Hoff. We spent a long time looking at the pictures that showed the insides of those houses.

The houses were stuffed with things: pictures and pieces of cloth and tall plants with feathery leaves, and lamps—so many lamps! Every table was covered with something. I couldn't see what the use of any of it was, except for the lamps, of course, but it seemed like there were way too many of those.

Mrs. Hoff said her mother's house was just like that, crowded with things that didn't have any use but that were pretty. "That's what people where I come from think is beautiful," she said.

I had never thought of a house as being a thing to decorate. The Yup'ik people decorated everything we made. Our wooden dishes were smoothed until they were silky, and then painted. It was the same with ladles and spoons, and needle cases and storage boxes. Even the most ordinary household things, like water buckets, had wonderfully carved handles. The designs and carvings of our belts and earrings and dance masks were all very beautiful. And no two were alike, because Yup'ik people didn't like to do the same thing over and over. But our houses had no decoration at all, so making a house beautiful was a new idea for me.

In the magazines there were pictures of animals we'd never seen before, like the cow. Mrs. Hoff explained that people kept as many cows as they could feed, and they took the cows' milk and put it into cans. Sometimes they made the milk into the butter and cheese that Mrs. Hoff had in other containers on her shelf. We had never tried butter and cheese and milk, but they didn't seem very interesting.

Another strange animal was the horse, which looked like a caribou without horns. A person got on its back to ride. I had a lot of questions about that. Why did the animal let him do that, and what did he do if the horse started to run fast, like caribou? Mr. Hoff told us stories about the days he spent breaking horses to the saddle. It sounded very exciting, but he said only boys could do it.

We laughed and laughed at the picture of pigs inside a fence. There couldn't be an animal funnier-looking than a pig, we thought. But later, after we'd seen pictures of many other animals, we knew we were wrong. There were a lot of animals funnier-looking than a pig.

Pigs were raised for their meat and they didn't run wild. When someone wanted meat, he didn't have to go hunting, because the animal was right there inside a fence next to where the person lived. Mr. Hoff liked to talk to us about that. If the village people wanted

to, we could keep animals that way, so we wouldn't
have to hunt. It was one of his favorite ideas for
civilizing us.

He really liked showing us children the pictures in
those magazines and explaining them to us. His face
would light up and his eyes would look so happy. I
think lots of the things were as amazing to him as they
were to us. There was a machine called a *telephone* that
let a person talk to another person who was far away.
Mr. Hoff had talked on a telephone, once. There were
lights that didn't need any oil or matches. That was
called *electricity*.

Mr. Hoff showed us pictures of bicycles. They were
very popular, he said. A bicycle was for riding on, like
a horse, and it had wheels that you had to make go
around by pushing with your feet. Some bicycles had
a very tall wheel in the front, and some had two wheels
the same size, and some bicycles had two seats so that
two people could ride at the same time.

The bicycles didn't interest Panruk and me very
much, but the moment Maklak saw them, he stopped
being interested in any of the other pictures and became

interested only in bicycles. He was crazy about them. He drew pictures of bicycles in the mud, and tried to talk Grandpa into building him one. It was all he talked about with his friends. Mr. Hoff tried to explain to him how a bicycle worked, but he couldn't explain how it kept from falling over. He said it was just something you had to do to understand, that was all.

After we'd been looking at those magazines for a few hours, we'd leave the Hoffs' house nearly dizzy with new ideas.

The world wasn't at all what we'd thought it was.

5 Summer

Summer was our busiest time of the year. The sun never set completely in the summer, so we could work all day and all night, too, if we needed to. We were getting ready for winter and we would be able to rest later, when it was too cold to hunt or fish.

Grandma got us up early in the morning while the birds were still sleeping, and we didn't stop working until late at night, when the low sun made all the trees look yellow.

And as hard as we worked all day, there was always time after our work was finished to play ball down by the river. We had balls made of woven grass filled with caribou fur. You had to keep the ball up in the air and not let it touch the ground.

Sometimes we played tag or hide-and-seek or

blindman's bluff, and even the women and old men played until we were all limp from laughing.

Mr. Hoff grumbled about our games. He said none of us got much sleep in the summer. He wouldn't let David come and play with us, even though I could see that David really wanted to.

But it didn't seem to matter how much sleep we got. We got all our work done, and we had a good time besides.

The first flowers had bloomed, and the woods and creek banks were full of pink roses and bluebells. I liked the roses best of all. Some of them were pale pink and some were medium, but the deep pink ones were my favorites. I wished I could take that color home with me and keep it all winter long, somehow.

The mosquitoes were thick by this time—the little fast ones with white stripes on their legs, the ones that made a mean zinging noise. But we children knew to not pay any attention to the mosquitoes. If we let them annoy us, we might go into a frenzy, the way caribou and dogs and other animals did when the mosquitoes tormented them, making their eyes and tender noses swell with bites.

The men put nets and fish traps into the river, and fished with dip nets and spears in the creeks. Fishing was the most important job we had all year. If we worked very hard, we could catch enough fish during the summer to last us all winter.

We women and girls cleaned and split the fish and hung them on racks to dry. We used every part of the fish. We hung the fish eggs inside their little egg pouches to dry, and Grandma chopped the king salmon tails into pieces and dried those to boil with the fish eggs. Grandma always dried the backbones, too—for dog food, she said, but she was the one who ate most of them. She loved them boiled and dipped in seal oil.

Even the fish skins were used. The aunts scraped the salmon skins, and Panruk and I rolled them up and took them to the cache. Later we would use them to make raincoats and boots for wet snow and rainy weather.

Auntie Nunagak put all the fish heads in grass bags. Then she buried them in a deep hole by our house.

We would eat them later in the summer when they had fermented.

David helped Auntie and me dig the hole for the fish heads. He was interested in everything we did, and came every chance he got to see what we were doing.

"When this fish is ready, you can have some," Auntie Nunagak said to David.

David looked at her sadly. "My father won't let me," he said.

"Why not?" I asked, surprised.

David looked uncomfortable. "He says that eating spoiled fish is disgusting."

Auntie Nunagak didn't say anything, just made a face to show what she thought of that. Rotten fish *smelled* terrible, but it was everyone's favorite thing to eat. Mine, too.

There were three main runs of salmon: the kings first, then the chums, and, last of all, the silver salmon. The silvers were the easiest because they came so late, we didn't have to cut them—we just buried them whole in grass-lined pits.

Everyone worried about rain in the summer, so we

watched the skies anxiously for dark clouds. Too much rain could ruin the drying fish, even when we covered the drying racks with grass mats. And if rain made the river too high, driftwood could get caught in our nets, and the traps wouldn't catch fish. Our shaman had died the year before, so the old men asked the shaman from the next village to come and do a special dance and song to keep the sun shining.

Inside the men's house, the shaman put his hands into his fish-skin parka and thrashed them around to make the dry, crackly skin of his parka rattle. Some of the children were frightened, and Panruk hid her face in her hands and watched him through her fingers. He sang while two drummers drummed, and then his eyes rolled back in his head and he shouted words none of us could understand. When he came to himself, he said that the weather would stay good for many more days.

Mr. Hoff hadn't heard that the shaman had come to keep the rain away until late in the afternoon, because he had been out in the woods, cutting birch. When he found out, he rushed down to the riverbank where the shaman was getting into his canoe to go back to his village. Mr. Hoff didn't look like himself at all. His eyes were wild, and his hair, full of wood chips, was standing up on end. He clutched his Bible tightly under his arm.

He stopped on the bank in front of the shaman and raised his Bible above his head with both hands. He began to pray loudly to his god to protect our village from the messenger of the devil. That's what he called the shaman. Then he fell on his knees and prayed some more.

The shaman seemed hardly to notice Mr. Hoff. Then, as he pushed his canoe off from the riverbank, he looked up at Mr. Hoff and disdainfully made a very rude gesture to him. That was all.

We were all so embarrassed at Mr. Hoff's bad manners that we lowered our eyes and walked away, leaving Mr. Hoff alone on the riverbank, red-faced and angry.

That was the first time we saw Mr. Hoff behave so badly, but it wasn't the last.

6 Trading

Late in the summer, after the salmon runs ended, my father and grandfather and uncle loaded up their canoes and went down to Bethel, near the mouth of the river. There they met the lower-river people, who had bags of seal oil and other things to trade. We had lots of furs because we lived in the woods, and the lower-river people had sea animals because they lived near the ocean. We each needed what the other had, so we were glad to trade with one another.

When the men were getting ready to go on their trading trip, Grandpa sent Panruk and me to the cache to count the furs into bundles. Furs were always tied in parka bundles for easy trading. Each bundle was enough for a man's parka—forty-five ground squirrel skins or thirty-three muskrat skins. We usually had some beaver and otter skins, along with caribou skins, sinew, and legs to trade as well. Caribou legs made good boots. Our men traded one bundle of parka furs for a small bag of seal oil, and two bundles and one set of caribou legs for a large bag of seal oil.

Iraluq and Taulan loaded the bundles into the canoes. Maklak was so excited to be going on his first trip with the men that he kept getting in their way. Finally Taulan took him by the back of his collar and the seat of his pants and put him up on the boat rack. "Don't move," said Taulan, very sternly.

Sometimes my father and grandfather came home with the stomach of a whale filled with the oil and blubber of the seal or the white whale. They'd save that for our winter festivals, when we'd be very proud to have such a fine gift to give away. They also traded for seal skins and walrus skins for boot bottoms, and for walrus rawhide, which made the strongest kind of rope.

Then they would take whatever furs they had left to the American trading post.

I asked Grandpa if he would bring me some pink

calico, the color of roses, from the trading post.

"I'll get some white," said Grandpa.

I knew he was just teasing me. "White is for old men!" I said. When the Russians first came to trade, they had only white cloth. So Grandpa and the other old men never used anything but white for their qaspeqs.

Grandpa laughed and said he'd look for pink.

"And Mamma," I said, "likes blue."

He made a face. "That's too much to remember," he said.

I knew the men would get shells for their rifles and matches and tobacco and tea. Iraluq and Taulan would get store pants, and there would be something for Maklak. You never could tell what. Once Grandpa brought Maklak an American harmonica, but Mamma took it away from him because it made too much noise.

While the men in our family were off trading, we women did the last of the summer work. We made bundles of dry grass, which we'd weave into baskets and socks and mats. We dug up the little roots Grandma called "mouse food," picked cotton grass for fire-starter, and gathered the rust-colored moss that made the best wicks for our lamps. Along the riverbank, we collected good pieces of driftwood to use as torches.

We also picked baskets of Labrador tea leaves. Labrador tea has a strong, sharp smell, and the wind carried that smell to you even when you were a long way from the tundra. The tea we made from the leaves tasted just like the smell.

Grandma and Mamma and the aunts were always so pleased when we had filled the cache with all these good things for winter. Sometimes Grandma would climb up the ladder to the cache and open the door and just look around, smiling.

"What are you looking for, Grandma?"

"Nothing," she would say. "I just like to look at everything."

I did, too.

Then, when the summer jobs were finished, Grandma and Mamma and the aunts began to mend all our clothes and sew new ones. Panruk and I sat with them to do the little sewing jobs, and to learn.

Only food was more important than good clothes.

Yup'ik children were shown from the time we were very small how to take good care of our clothes. We had to beat the snow and frost off our outdoors clothes and put them to dry on the racks near the door. If our clothes became wet, we let them freeze and then beat the frost out of them.

We had to be careful not to let our boots dry too fast, or they'd become stiff. We had to show Grandma any bloodstains or grease stains on our clothes so that they could be rubbed out with snow. Dirty clothes didn't keep you warm, she said.

But even with good care, everyone in the family needed at least two new sets of clothes a year—summer clothes and winter clothes.

Before any sewing was done, the skins were soaked in urine to get the fat off, then stretched and scraped and dried and softened by twisting and rubbing. Sinew was prepared and twisted, needles were made, and our knives were sharpened so we could cut the skins.

Panruk and I each had been given our own sewing

kit and a woman's knife—an *uluaq*—when we were little. Grandma said a woman would be gray before she had learned everything she needed to know to be a master seamstress. Sewing was a very complicated art.

Iraluq and Taulan came back from the trading trip wearing new store pants, and Maklak had an American hat. He was very proud of that hat, even though it was so big that it slid down and covered his eyes. He kept pushing it up and jamming it hard on top of his head.

I looked at Grandpa to see if he'd remembered the pink calico. He made the sort of face that meant that he knew what I was looking for, but that he hadn't found quite the thing I'd wanted.

After everything was put away in the cache, Grandpa showed us what he'd gotten in trade at the American store. There was a piece of calico with blue and white squares. That was for Mamma. There was a big piece with all kinds of different colored stripes for everyone else. And for me there was calico with a yellow background and pale pink flowers. It wasn't the same as plain dark pink, but it was beautiful just the same, so I smiled at Grandpa.

Later that night, Taulan and Iraluq came to our house and told us the news from downriver. They said the Yup'ik people from the lower river looked different from us. Their legs were shorter and their faces seemed broader. Their speech was different, too, as if they talked through their noses. Taulan and Iraluq tried to talk like the Bethel people and made us all laugh.

They told us how everyone was afraid of the American soldiers. The United States Army had built a big fort at St. Michael, and sometimes they sent out soldiers to the villages. When the soldiers came to Bethel, the people sent all the big boys to hide. Every-one was afraid they were going to take their boys into the army. Taulan and Iraluq said they would have run, too, if they'd seen any soldiers!

I wouldn't have run. I would have liked very much to see those American soldiers.

There was a lot I wanted to see.

7 Pockets

Every day after the middle of summer, Grandma
would send Panruk and me out into the tundra to
see how the berries were coming along.

Some years there were lots of berries and some
years there weren't. Some years the berries were big
and sweet, and sometimes they were little and sour.
You never could tell until they were ripe.

The lovely pale orange salmonberries were ready
first. Grandma used them right away to make *akutaq*
because unlike other berries, salmonberries couldn't
be kept for a long time. There was nothing we liked
better than akutaq. First Grandma put a handful of
caribou tallow in the big pottery bowl, and with her
hand she whipped the tallow until it was soft. Then
she added seal oil and the berries and kept mixing it

with her hand until it was fluffy, and such a beautiful color. In the winter she used other berries and put snow in it to make it cold, but we liked it warm, too. Akutaq was rich and sweet and oily, and it melted on your tongue. It was delicious.

Next the blueberries were ripe, and then the bright glossy red cranberries, and last to ripen were the high-bush cranberries. When it was time, all the women in our village went to the berry patches and picked from early in the morning until late at night.

Sometimes it drizzled and was foggy while we picked. We could hardly see each other in the low mist as we spread out over the tundra, which was wet and full of little bog holes waiting to trip us up. But we didn't care. We wanted to have akutaq and berries all winter, so we kept picking.

Every evening when we got back to the village, Mamma and the aunts cleaned the twigs out of the berries, and then they sewed the berries into fish-skin bags to store in the cache. They left out enough for the men, and every night Panruk and I took a bowl of fresh berries to the men's house for Grandpa and the others. The men were happy to have them and sent their thanks to all the berry pickers.

We picked extra for Mrs. Hoff. She needed lots of berries for the ten boys who were coming to the Hoffs' school, so she paid us in tea and flour and sugar and matches for every basket of berries we brought to her.

That summer, Mr. and Mrs. Hoff hired a lot of people from Bethel and other places to work for them. Mr. Hoff sent boats up and down the river to buy dried fish for the school. He also bought rafts full of firewood for their stove and spruce logs for lumber to finish the schoolroom.

Mr. Hoff hired men to cut boards from those logs. They used long saws. The man at the top of the sawing frame pulled up and the man on the bottom pulled down. The man on the bottom was always covered with sawdust, so I thought it was better to be on top.

Mr. Hoff had a *Kodak*. That was a box that could make a picture just like the pictures Mrs. Hoff had hanging on the wall. After Mr. Hoff pointed the Kodak at something, he would take the film into a room in his house and wash it with special water, and then there would be the picture of the thing he'd pointed at.

Mr. Hoff took a lot of pictures of the workmen sawing logs and building the school. He said he wanted to have pictures of "before" and "after"—before there was any house or school, and after everything was built. The pictures were for his church in Maryland.

Mrs. Hoff got some of the older women from our village to work for her, those who had lots of help at home and could get away during the busy summer work. She taught some to bake bread, and some how to clean in her way—scrubbing the wooden floors and washing the dishes and steel pots.

We were very surprised to learn that everything the Hoffs wore had to be washed in soap and water, boiled in a big tub, and then scrubbed up and down on the scrub board. It was very hard work. I think the Hoffs used as much water in one day as we used in the whole summer. It was David's job to bring water from the river in the wagon, many buckets a day.

After the clothes were washed on the scrub board and hung to dry in the sun, Mrs. Hoff had to iron them. She heated the iron on the big stove and pressed the cloth with the iron to make the cloth smooth. She tried to teach the women who helped her to do this, but it was no use. They didn't like the heavy hot iron, and they just couldn't see the use of taking the wrinkles out of the cloth.

Mrs. Hoff was getting ready for the boys who would come to school. No Yup'ik family would send their boys to school, so all the students would be orphan boys, children no one cared about. Kasruq, the orphan who lived in our men's house, would be going to the Hoffs' school.

Orphans in Yup'ik villages had a hard life. No

women brought them food. They ate what was left over when the other men had finished eating. Their clothes were castoffs that they had to mend themselves. And they had to take orders from everyone.

Kasruq was a little older than Iraluq. He didn't call any attention to himself, but I had the feeling he would grow up to be a strong man, even if no one cared for him now. But Mr. Hoff cared for him, because he wanted him to come to his school. I thought it must be nice for Kasruq to be noticed by Mr. Hoff when no one else paid much attention to him.

Because the boys coming to the school were orphans, they didn't have much in the way of clothes to bring with them. So Mrs. Hoff ordered cloth pants and shirts and boots to be sent on the mission boat with the rest of the supplies.

Mrs. Hoff had bought bundles of skins to make a parka for each boy, and she hired Cakayak's grandma and Uliggaq's grandma and my grandma to sew the parkas. They were the very best sewers in our village, and the very fastest, too.

And then Mrs. Hoff asked if we girls could come to

work as well. Since most of the summer work was done, Grandma said I could go to help in the kitchen, and Panruk could go to work on the parkas.

When we came to work, Mrs. Hoff made us take baths in her big galvanized tub and wash our hair with soap to make sure there were no lice in it. Mrs. Hoff hated lice worse than anything in the world, and after David had been visiting in an ena or the men's house, Mrs. Hoff would ruffle through his hair, frowning, while David made funny faces at me over her shoulder.

The other thing Mrs. Hoff hated was strong smell— raw, wet caribou skins being scraped or made into rawhide and dried fish and rotten fish heads all gave her a terrible headache. She couldn't go into the men's house at all, because of the strong smells. We were used to the smells and hardly noticed them.

She gave those of us who worked in her house cloth dresses because it was so hot inside the house that even our summer parkas were too heavy. The Hoffs always had the fire going, except in the hottest month, even if they weren't cooking. Grandpa said a log house wasn't as warm as a sod house because it was above

ground and the wind hit it. We didn't keep fire in
our houses all the time. Even in the coldest part of
winter, our sod houses were warm without fire, because
of the warmth of the people inside and because of the
oil lamp.

We each had a long shirt to wear under our dress,
some very short pants made of white cloth, and a
white apron to tie over our dresses so they wouldn't
get dirty. Each apron had a *pocket*, a little bag sewn
onto the apron. You could put almost anything in a
pocket and carry it around so easily. I thought pockets
were a good idea.

When we left at the end of the day, we would put
our regular clothes back on. I was glad to put my parka
back on, but I missed the pocket. I asked Grandma
why we couldn't have pockets in our clothes, but she
didn't say anything.

So Panruk and Grandma and I each had a new
dress and a white apron and our hair washed with
soap. My hair felt sleek, like the beaver fur when the
guard hairs have been plucked, and it shone the same
way in the mirror. I liked the way it looked so much

that I didn't have to be asked to wash my hair any-more, but Mrs. Hoff often sent me to wash my hands.

Yup'ik children were told to get our hands dirty to keep away illness, because the dirt would make a path for the illness to leave us. But Mrs. Hoff told us that we must keep our hands clean or we would get sick and make others around us sick.

I asked Grandma what we should do about this rule, and she said we would keep our hands clean while we were at the Hoffs', but when we came home we should rub our hands in the dirt in the yard outside our house.

8 Questions

One day, in a boatload of goods for the mission, there was the sewing machine Mrs. Hoff had been telling us about. Mr. Hoff took it out of its wooden box and put it together, and then the three grandmas and Panruk and I gathered around to watch Mrs. Hoff work the machine.

It was black and shiny, so shiny we could see our faces in it. There was a little board at the bottom called the *treadle* that she put her feet on to move the needle up and down. The noise that the treadle made—*rackety, rackety*—was horrible, and Panruk and Grandma covered their ears. While Mrs. Hoff was pumping, she pushed the material through the needle to the back, and there was a straight seam, with every stitch the same size.

Mrs. Hoff said she could make a cotton dress in just a few hours with this machine, but there were still some things that had to be sewn by hand. That was hemming. Even though I didn't sew as well as Panruk, Mrs. Hoff would sometimes set me to hemming things with a shiny needle and cotton thread. Cotton thread was much easier to use than caribou sinew because you could get a nice long thread from the spool. But that thread was not as strong as caribou sinew, and sometimes the seams would come apart or the thread would rot.

Sometimes the needle on the sewing machine would break and then Mrs. Hoff would become very cross, and her face would grow red and her hair would come loose from the braids, as it always did when things were not going well. In some ways, I thought the Yup'ik way of sewing was better.

While we were all sewing in the big room, Mrs. Hoff would talk to us about how we were heathens and what we must do to become civilized. She and Mr. Hoff had come to live with us to teach us right from wrong and to help us get to heaven. Mr. Hoff had said what hell was like, but we hadn't heard much about heaven. David and I had talked about it, but he didn't know what went on there. So I thought I'd ask her.

"Mrs. Hoff," I said, "what is it like in heaven?"

"Well," said Mrs. Hoff. She frowned.

"The Bible doesn't really say," she said at last. "But I'm sure it's very nice. And better than hell."

I couldn't believe she didn't know what it was like. After all, the Hoffs were always talking about trying to get us to go there.

"David told me that there would be a lot of singing there," I said.

"People say that," she said. "But I don't think it talks about singing in the Bible."

"Well, if there was singing, would it be white man's singing, or Yup'ik singing?" I asked.

"I should think that people in heaven would have just the kind of singing they liked best," she said.

I didn't see how that would work, because if people were singing different things at the same time, it would be awful, but I didn't want to ask any more because Grandma and the other women were giving me looks.

In the Yup'ik way, it's very bad to hurt somebody's mind, confuse them, or contradict them. Mrs. Hoff was uncomfortable with my questions, so I was hurting her mind. I was sorry, but I had so many questions that they just popped out sometimes.

Mrs. Hoff said we could all have English names when we were baptized.

In the Yup'ik way, there were not different names for boys and girls. Babies were named for the last person in the village who died, whether it was a man or a woman. Then the person who had died was born again in the new baby, and the family of the dead person treated the baby as if he or she were a relative, the dead one born again. Mrs. Hoff said that was a heathen belief.

I was named for Teksik's baby girl who had died, and so Teksik sewed me beautiful beaver mitts and her husband made me earrings, because I was like their little girl again.

We were all very quiet when Mrs. Hoff talked about names. It would make people very unhappy to have to believe in Mrs. Hoff's way—that their relatives were gone forever and could not come back.

I liked the Hoffs, but I didn't really understand their ideas.

When I left the Hoffs' house, I saw Grandpa sitting on top of the men's house. Grandpa was the only one who didn't mind my questions. I knew he was watching out for driftwood, because the river had risen and it would have swept up some of the logs lying on the banks far upriver. If he saw a good log go by, he would call out, and someone would jump into a canoe and drag the log to the bank to use later.

Grandpa was carving a wooden ladle while he watched. His tool kit was spread out next to him, along with his little box of dye. His dye box was made of wood, which he'd painted red. On the cover were carved strange little figures and men, and the cover slid on and off on little tracks.

I had always loved that box, and he used to let me play with it and put the cover on and take it off. But now that I was almost a woman, I knew I shouldn't touch his things anymore, because it might give him bad luck. Grandpa was using a curved knife to scoop the wood out of the ladle, a little bit at a time, and a pile of shavings sat on his lap. He looked very peaceful, so I thought it was a good time to ask him about hell.

"Grandpa," I said, "Mrs. Hoff said that only people who believe in their religion can go to heaven, and the rest go to hell. So that means that everyone who has already died in our village went to hell."

Grandpa just kept on carving and he didn't look at me. That meant he was listening hard.

"That just doesn't seem fair," I said. "If their god wanted everyone to go to heaven, why didn't he come to people and just tell them what he wanted, and speak in Yup'ik? Why did he wait so long to tell people about heaven? Why didn't he tell them right away, at the beginning of people, so no one would have to go to hell?"

Grandpa stopped carving and looked at me.

"I don't know, Minuk," he said.

Panruk and I went to help Mrs. Hoff every day except Sunday, and I began to learn English from listening to David and Mr. and Mrs. Hoff. It wasn't very hard to learn, but there were a lot of things both Mr. and Mrs. Hoff said all the time that were hard to understand—like "Merciful heavens!" and "Goodness gracious," which Mrs. Hoff said all the time, and "By jingo!" which Mr. Hoff said very often.

David always explained those expressions. I asked David if he would speak to me in English instead of Yup'ik so that I could learn faster, and he was very pleased to do that. I think it made him feel very grown-up to be teaching English words to a big girl.

9 *Lessons*

When it was almost time for summer to end, when
there were yellow leaves on the birch and cottonwood
trees, and the berry leaves had turned scarlet, and the
whole tundra smelled of highbush cranberries, it was
time for the Berry Festival.

First the men cleaned the qasgiq. They hung new
grass hangings over the mask room, and sanded rough
places in the benches, and fixed the water bucket.
They polished the stone bowls of the oil lamps and
cleaned the black bear skin that covered the door.
Then the qasgiq was ready for the festival.

The women brought big wooden bowls full of berries
mashed and mixed with seal oil into the men's house.
They set the bowls on the benches behind the firepit,
which was covered with planks so we could dance.

All the young girls in our village lined up in our best clothes to do the berry dance, which began the festival. Two of the old men drummed for us, and we danced a joyful dance because we'd gotten so many berries, and because the summer fishing had been so good, and because our caches were full of food for the winter. We didn't move our feet when we danced, the way the men did, but we bent our knees in rhythm to the drums, and we twisted the top part of our bodies to show how we'd picked the berries, to show how a mother bear and her cubs had gone away from the berry patch when we came, and to show how our mothers would make akutaq from the berries when the winter came.

Then the women brought in platters full of fish and

willow grouse, and we ate everything and had a good time together. And that was the end of summer.

The wind was blowing the last of the leaves off the trees and bushes, all the paths were filled with fallen leaves, and there was ice at the edges of the puddles. The men set their blackfish traps in the lakes, and when they pulled the traps out of the water, they tipped the blackfish out onto the ground and let them freeze. Then they put them by the hundreds into fish-skin bags and stored them in the cache for the dogs.

This was the time to get whitefish from the lakes and river, before the ice started to run in the river.

Whitefish were put into grass bags and buried in deep holes, so they could be eaten frozen. The oil was carefully saved. People liked whitefish oil even more than seal oil, and our women would be ashamed to have a festival without a lot of whitefish oil to serve to our visitors.

Everything was almost ready for the school, and the

boys would soon arrive from all the villages. I really wanted to see what a school was like. I asked Grandpa, but he didn't know, for he'd never seen one.

A lot of people were worried that the boys who were coming to the school would not be good providers. That was because they would be eating the Hoffs' food, and white people used salt in their food. The old men said that the animals wouldn't come to you if you ate too much salt. Besides that, while those boys were going to the school, they wouldn't be learning in the men's house.

In the men's house, every day the men talked to the boys about the things they must know to live their lives properly, just as they sometimes talked to the girls.

The boys had to be very quiet in the men's house. They had to listen very hard and memorize what the men told them. Knowledge is like a seed, they were told, that grows larger and blossoms over the years. And knowledge is the only thing of value that no one can take from you. The boys were shown hundreds of things about hunting and fishing, and how to make tools, and how to take care of themselves in the woods and on the river.

The boys were ridiculed for lying down in the men's house because it was bad to sleep too much. It was shameful to the men to have the women get up before them. In the morning they must jump up and go outside right away to see what the weather was. In that way they would never be sick, and they would be ready for whatever work they must do that day.

The boys could not drink water. Instead, they dipped a feather into water and squeezed it into their mouths. If they drank too much water, their flesh would not be firm, and when food was short they would grow thin rapidly.

They must keep the snow removed from the ena passageways when the wind piled drifts across the doorways. They must keep the water holes clear of ice. They must keep the village clean by removing trash and refuse. These cleared paths would let the animals come to them. And the men must think about the animals all the time, because the animals that lived in the spirit world knew what the men did and what they thought. The animals would only come to someone who thought about them in the right way.

A good hunter who shared with everyone and who spoke wisely and quietly in the men's house was "a man indeed."

In the Yup'ik way, whatever you did must be for the good of the whole village, not just good for yourself. In this way we could all survive the hard times, and we could have many good times.

There were many, many rules for living life in the Yup'ik way, and our elders talked to us constantly, showing us the things we should do and the things we shouldn't.

That was our school, which was very different from the missionaries' school.

10 *Panruk*

One day not long after the Berry Festival, Panruk didn't feel well, so she didn't go with me to the Hoffs' to sew that day. When I came back to the house late in the afternoon, I found that Grandma had lowered one of the grass mats that hung over the bench against the back wall. From the look on her face, I knew that Panruk was behind it.

Panruk had become a woman.

Of course, I had known that it would happen to her. I knew it would happen to me, as well. But knowing something will happen and having it actually happen are not the same. I felt a terrible pain in my throat when I stared at that grass curtain. My cousin, my friend, my playmate for all of my life! There would now be so many things we couldn't do together anymore.

I pulled aside the curtain and knelt beside Panruk as she lay on the bench, her eyes wide open. I took her hand and held it.

She looked at me and smiled, not afraid or sad, but content, the way she always was. Panruk accepted everything, questioned nothing, and was as sweet and patient as our mothers and aunts. I was the only one who asked too many questions and thought too many thoughts.

When a young girl first menstruated, there were rules. These rules were so strict that no one would dare break them, because breaking them would affect everyone in the village.

For ten days Panruk could not sit down or walk around. When she was tired she could lie down, but she must not sit. Not once. After ten days of that, she had to sit still in a dark corner of the house dressed in an old parka. She could have water only once in the morning and once in the evening, and that she had to suck from a feather.

After another ten days, Panruk was allowed to stand up. Grandma went to the passageway where we cooked and got a handful of ashes, which she threw behind Panruk. Grandma said the ashes fell on Panruk's pathway and cut off her past. There was no way to become a child again.

I didn't want to be a child anymore, either, if Panruk couldn't be a child with me.

Panruk bathed and dressed in a new qaspeq with a hood and belt, which she must wear always. She had to be completely covered, both indoors and out, with special fish-skin mittens without thumbs, and boots—even in summer, when we usually went barefoot.

The other girls in the village were told that Panruk was standing up, that she was a woman.

As a woman, Panruk had to give away her doll and everything else she'd owned as a girl—even her lovely earrings, which our grandfather had made for her, and even her sewing kit. Grandma and the aunts had gifts of needles and needle cases ready to give to the rest of the girls to celebrate the end of Panruk's childhood.

Of course, Panruk gave her doll to me, but it made me very sad to think that Panruk and I would never play together again, that we would never again go into that imaginary world we lived in when we played with our dolls.

I had played dolls with Cakayak and sometimes with Uliggaq, but neither of them was very good at pretending. So I knew that I, too, wouldn't be playing much with dolls anymore.

Last of all, Panruk was tattooed. Most tattoos were three lines fanning out under the bottom lip down to the bottom of the chin. Grandpa said women at the mouth of the river had different tattoos, and he had seen some women with beautifully designed tattoos on their cheeks. Grandma thought that sounded gaudy, but I wished I could see those cheek tattoos.

Grandma prepared a long string, which she coated with soot, and then she made a hole in the skin under

Panruk's lip, by the corner of her mouth. Then slowly she drew the string through the top layer of skin to make a dark line, which looked blue when it was finished. Panruk said it didn't hurt much, but it took a long time. Sometimes the string had to be pulled through twice or three times because the mark it left wasn't dark enough. We weren't supposed to cry when we were tattooed, but I was afraid that I wouldn't be as brave as Panruk.

Of course, I would be as proud as everyone else to be tattooed—to be a woman—but I wondered why boys didn't have to endure any traditions like that.

But then, they were not unclean, like women.

When Panruk was allowed to go outside again, she couldn't look off into the distance. She could take only little short glances so that she would not go blind in her old age. She could not drink while she was stooping over, or eat birds that fly south in the winter, or handle the soil.

For a year she would have restrictions. She couldn't hunt for eggs. She couldn't pick berries, or they'd fall early. She couldn't go in a boat, or the fish would go away from our village. She couldn't cook or prepare skins for the whole year. What she did was very important for the entire village. If there was bad weather or poor hunting and fishing, she would be blamed for not following the rules.

For the rest of her life, men must not breathe in her bad air when they passed her, or have direct eye contact. She had to be very careful with men's clothing and not leave hers lying around, for a woman was thought to have bad emanations that offended the animals.

The shaman told us once about a time he had gone to the spirit world to visit the souls of the animals who had been killed in the previous year. Some of the animals said that the hunter who had caught them had treated them with great respect, and that they would willingly allow that same hunter to catch them again. But some of the animals said that they would not go again to the hunter who had killed them because he was careless in his relations with women, and the animals often had to endure the stink of women.

I felt humiliated when I heard that. It was very hard to be thought responsible for bad hunting and the accidents that sometimes happened.

After Panruk could stand and walk around, she went with me to visit the Hoffs again.

We were alone with Mrs. Hoff, who was hemming an apron. As she worked, she asked Panruk questions about the Yup'ik way of becoming a woman. After listening a bit, Mrs. Hoff said that our traditions were superstitions and that she didn't approve of them.

Then she suddenly put her needle down and looked at the picture on the wall that had been taken when she was a young girl. "When I became a woman, I had to put my hair on top of my head for the first time. It couldn't be worn down and loose anymore," she said. "And I had to put away my short skirts and put on long skirts. And the corset."

Mrs. Hoff was quiet for a minute. Then she smiled at us and said, "My head ached for weeks from the pins I used to fasten my hair up. And I kept tripping over

my new long skirts. And oh, how I hated the corsets."
She shook herself a little and said, "Of course, I got
used to all of that. But still, it was hard at first."

I think Mrs. Hoff felt sympathy for the changes
Panruk had to make, too.

Girls had so much to endure.

Qanrilaq's family spoke to Grandpa about Panruk.
He and Grandma asked Panruk if she had any objection
to Qanrilaq as a husband, and Panruk just put her
head down and shook her head.

I had an objection to Qanrilaq. When he hadn't
been long in the men's house, he was mean to us little
girls. He threw rocks at us and bothered us. Of course,
he was not a little boy anymore, and my father said he
was a good hunter, but I remembered his mean little
eyes as he tormented us. And now when we saw him
in the men's house, or going about his business, he
didn't smile. He didn't laugh and joke with the other
boys and men.

I didn't like him. I wished someone else had asked
for Panruk.

After Panruk agreed to Qanrilaq, the women in
his family started making new clothes for Panruk: a
beautiful muskrat-belly parka, caribou boots, a beaded
belt, and lovely fawn-skin mittens. They would bring
those clothes to Panruk, who would put them on and
take a meal to Qanrilaq in the qasgiq, and so he would
become her husband.

"Grandfather," I said, "I don't like Qanrilaq. He
never smiles."

"He's a good hunter," said Grandfather.

"I like people who smile," I said.

"Well, he's not to become your husband," he said.

"He used to be mean when he was a boy," I said.

"I remember," said Grandfather thoughtfully.

"Maybe he's still mean," I said.

"In that case, Panruk can throw him away," said
Grandfather. "I myself had two wives before your
grandmother, and she had one husband before me.
No one suited us until we married each other."

That was true, I knew. Panruk need not stay with

anyone she wasn't suited to. What I worried about was whether Panruk would ever think to complain. Perhaps she would be so good and so sweet that she wouldn't hold herself valuable.

11 *School*

David got very sick before the snow came, and he
stayed in bed, coughing and making a bad sound in his
throat. When I took him the breakfast his mother had
cooked for him, he didn't want to eat. I stayed with
him by his bed as long as I could, because I liked to
talk to David. He took his job of teaching me English
very seriously, and even though he didn't eat, he asked
me to tell him the names of everything on his
breakfast tray, and corrected me if I made a mistake.

After David had been sick for a while, Grandma and
the women who were sewing with Mrs. Hoff said that
she should call for the shaman from the next village.
Mrs. Hoff became very angry.

"Haven't I told you, and hasn't Mr. Hoff told you,
that the shamans are evil and you should have nothing

to do with them? Not until you've stopped listening to these terrible men will you be able to live the good life we've told you about."

Cakayak's grandmother was so worried about David that she kept trying. "He can help your boy. Evil spirits made him sick and the shaman will pull them out." She jerked an imaginary spirit up in the air to show how the shaman would do it.

"We have medicine here that will help him," said Mrs. Hoff, her lips set in a straight line. "He would be dead before I would ever consult a shaman."

I knew that no one would talk about the shaman again to Mrs. Hoff, just as they wouldn't talk to her about names and other things she'd shown disapproval of. They would just do what they wanted to do without telling her, because she got so upset.

The Hoffs did have good medicine, and many of the grown-ups went to them for help when they were sick. Everyone liked the cough medicine the best, because it tasted good and made your stomach feel warm.

Grandpa felt that Mr. and Mrs. Hoff had more power over sickness than the shaman did. That's why he listened thoughtfully to what Mr. Hoff had to say. If the Hoffs were right about medicine, maybe they were right about other things as well.

And David did get better after a while.

By late fall, the workers had finished the big room that would be used for the school and the rooms upstairs where the boys would live. Then Mr. Hoff got out the tin buckets of paint that he had kept in the storage room. We'd never seen wall paint before. Mr. Hoff used the paint to cover the boards on the inside of the classroom. I helped him put on two coats of paint. Mr. Hoff got a lot all over himself, but I was as careful as if it were seal oil and didn't splash a drop.

The room was beautiful when we were finished, and the walls were so white that when the sun shone into the school, it hurt your eyes.

On one wall was a big board made of slate, which Mr. Hoff could write on, and there was a clock with numbers on it. Mr. Hoff told me how the clock divided the day into parts. When the hands were on certain numbers, the boys would come to the classroom and sit in their seats. Then, when the hands went around some more, it would be time for the boys to go to the kitchen to eat their lunch. Every time the hands moved, there was a certain thing to be done at a certain number. I felt tight all over when he explained it to me, as if a clock could tie you up and keep you from moving freely. I didn't think I liked the clock at all.

There was a picture of Benjamin Harrison, who was the president of the United States, and a wooden sign with letters in black and gold paint. "God is Love," Mr. Hoff said the sign said.

I looked at the sign for a minute, and then I said, "Mr. Hoff, if your god is love, why does he make people burn in hell?"

Mr. Hoff got his stern look. "That's the punishment for not believing," he said.

"Burning someone doesn't seem to be love," I said.

"You will understand, I'm sure, when you've had further instruction in religion," said Mr. Hoff.

"The old people say that we can be punished after we die," I said. "When we're on the path to the good place, we go through the villages of the animals. The first village is the dogs' village. If you have been cruel to dogs in your lifetime, the dogs will come out and hit you with sticks, to show you what it was like to live with bad humans."

Mr. Hoff looked at me. "I never heard that belief," he said.

"Does your religion teach people to be good to animals?"

"No," said Mr. Hoff. I knew that Mr. Hoff was very fond of his dogs and had names for all of them, and he treated them like children, really. So perhaps he was sorry that there weren't rules in his Bible about animals.

"Yup'ik people believe that you must be good to animals," I said. "And even trees and plants."

Mr. Hoff went back to his writing and didn't answer me. But I think he could feel me still looking at him because he cleared his throat and looked at the ceiling. "There are many things about life which are not explained in the Bible. But we know that God has a plan for us, and we must believe that everything will be for the best. We must have faith."

"Oh," I said. I had been thinking about faith a lot since the Hoffs came. What faith was, I could see, was not asking hard questions or looking at things too closely.

It was sometimes hard to believe things you were supposed to believe, so you needed help from other people. That was why people wanted you to believe what they believed, and why they didn't want you to ask questions. It was hard to believe that the shaman went under the water to the animal spirits, and it was hard to believe that the animal spirits didn't like the smell of women. It was hard to believe that there was a good place to go to after you die. But the more people who believed those things, the easier it was for you to believe them, too.

And if you wanted to believe, you had to pretend a little, the way we pretended that the animal masks in our plays were real animals. If you were saying to yourself, *That's Iraluq holding the beaver mask he made, and he's pretending to eat willow,* the play wouldn't be any fun. You must agree in your mind not to see what really is.

That's how both Mr. Hoff and our old people had faith.

12 Boots

The boys came to school in the big mission boat just before the river froze over for the winter. They didn't look very happy. I suppose they were better off coming to Mr. Hoff's school, but I don't think they all thought so. I think some of them would have been happier learning in the men's house.

Mrs. Hoff cut the hair of each orphan very short. The boys were very unhappy about that, because all their lives they'd been told that they would get sick if their hair was cut. Mrs. Hoff said that was just a heathen superstition. She said that it was the rule in her religion that the women have long hair and the men have short hair.

The Yup'ik men who lived along the coast shaved all the hair from the crown of their heads and left a

fringe of hair all around. Our men along the upper
Kuskokwim River kept their hair long all over.
Mr. and Mrs. Hoff did not approve of that.

"Why does your god want men to have short hair?"
I asked Mrs. Hoff.

Mrs. Hoff gave me the same look that grown-ups
often gave me because of the questions I asked, as if
she thought I was being annoying on purpose. "In the
first place, you shouldn't say 'your god' in that way.
He's everyone's God, not just mine."

"Yes, Mrs. Hoff," I said. "Why does god want men
to have short hair?" I asked again.

"Well, I'm sure there's a reason," said Mrs. Hoff.
"I just can't recall what it is now, I'm so busy. Ask
Mr. Hoff, will you?"

This was the way it was in our village, too. Sometimes I asked Grandma or Mamma or my father why
something was done, and they said, "I don't know," or
"It's always been done that way." Those answers never
pleased me. Having a question without an answer is
like having a mosquito bite that won't quit itching.

Each boy at the school was given a white shirt

and blue pants with suspenders. The boys looked so
different dressed in white man's clothes and with their
hair clipped short and their faces shining that we just
stared at them. Kasruq didn't look like himself at all.
He was so much thinner than he'd looked in his Eskimo
clothes. The boys all spent a lot of time looking at
themselves in the mirror, as if they couldn't believe
the change themselves. They had underclothes as well,
a suit to sleep in, knit socks, and, last of all, thick
leather white man's boots.

The day that Mr. and Mrs. Hoff passed out the boots
to the boys was not a good one.

Everything about white people was loud—their
voices, their saws, their cooking, the clanging metal
pots slamming on the iron stove, the lids of the stove
crashing down when wood was put into it, steel spoons
grating while they stirred, and the clatter of the metal
dishpans and slop buckets. They made a dozen different
kinds of noise all the time, but noisiest of all were
these boots.

Ten boys with ten pairs of boots stomping on wooden
floors! The boys had never worn anything but skin

boots, and they didn't know how to walk in them. All of us sewing in the big front room were disturbed all day.

At the end of that noisy day, the boys ran up the wooden stairs to their room and the noise of those boots on the stairs was so loud that Grandma put her hands over her ears and burst into tears. She said she wasn't coming back to work at the Hoffs' anymore, because everything was too loud.

Mrs. Hoff was very sympathetic and called up to the boys that they must walk more quietly, but Grandma folded up her sewing kit and left anyway.

At the end of the day, each boy had blisters on his feet.

I was glad I would never have to wear such big, clumsy boots.

When the boys didn't do what Mr. Hoff wanted, he would give them a whipping with a wide leather strap he kept hanging on a nail. The first time this happened, everyone was very quiet.

In the Yup'ik way you didn't punish a child, you talked to him and explained why his behavior was

bad for the people, and for himself. Sometimes the
boys who slept too long in the men's house were
dragged to the floor, but they were never struck. We
were all dismayed by Mr. Hoff's bad behavior.

Those first weeks were very hard for the boys.
They had to stay in the house all day, even though
they had been raised to spend most of every day outdoors. They had to wash themselves every morning,
and once a week they had to take a bath in the big
galvanized tub. One boy got a rash from the yellow
soap, and the youngest one cried bitterly when he
got soap in his eyes.

Mr. Hoff began to teach the boys to speak English,
and I was proud that I already understood so many
English words.

When Mr. Hoff began to teach the boys to read,
I would stand outside the schoolroom door and listen
to him whenever I could manage it. Around the
walls of the classroom, he had put a long paper with
big letters on it. He taught the boys the name of
each letter and the sound that each one stood for.
I memorized the letters, too, and all the words he

wrote on the big board. I wrote them in the snow with a stick when I left the Hoffs'.

But sometimes it was hard to find time to listen to the reading lessons. I was afraid I'd miss something important.

One afternoon, after all the boys had left school and had gone outdoors to do their chores, I stood in the schoolroom door and watched Mr. Hoff write the lessons for the next day on the board.

"Mr. Hoff, will you teach me to read?" I asked.

He looked at me with concern. "Oh, dear, no," he said. "That would not be a good idea at all," he said.

"Is reading just for boys, then?" I asked.

"No, of course not," he said. "But if you learned to read, you might think yourself above the boy who will marry you. And perhaps a young man would not want to take a woman who could read as a wife."

"Why not?" I asked.

"Well, it says in the Bible that the man must be the head of the family."

It was that way with our people as well. Maybe I wouldn't be a good wife if I learned to read. Maybe

I wouldn't be modest.

I nodded at him to show him that I understood what he said and then left the room. But I was going to learn to read anyway. Once I knew that the marks meant something, I couldn't bear not knowing what they said. I would teach myself, and no one would have to know. It would be my secret.

As the days grew colder, there was less daylight each day. When the sun came up late in the morning, it just peeked over the top of the hills and hung there, staining the clouds and snow and thick-frosted trees pink. Then it slipped back down behind the hills again.

This was the time of rest for our people.

Some wood had to be chopped for the men's house, water had to be brought from the water hole in the river, and the dogs had to be fed, but besides sewing, there was not much else that had to be done.

In the qasgiq, the men did woodworking and played

darts and string games. The boys played with their tops on the floorboards. One of their favorite games was to see if they could dash out of the qasgiq, go around it once, and get back inside before the top stopped spinning.

We girls liked to play storyknives, making pictures in the clean, fresh snow. We used our knives in the mud and dirt in the summertime, but I liked the squeak of the cold dry snow when I cut through the packed layers with my knife. One of us would take her knife and begin a story, drawing the pictures as she talked. Panruk made wonderful pictures with the storyknife, so sometimes I told the story and she drew the pictures. Most of us told the old stories that we'd learned from our elders, but I liked to make up new ones, too.

The day that Mr. Hoff told me I couldn't learn to read, I made up a story about a girl who had a secret magic power. She kept the magic in a little fish-skin bag that she wore around her neck. When she needed the magic, she'd wait until everyone was gone. Then she'd take it out of the bag and hold it in her hands so that she could see things far away and know things that had happened long ago. She became so wise that the people thought she was a shaman, and even the men asked her for help and advice.

All the girls liked that story a lot and asked for it often.

13 *Speeches*

Before the river froze over completely, Panruk
took the clothes Qanrilaq's family had made for her
to the men's house and left them in a pile in front
of Qanrilaq. That meant that she didn't want to be
married to him anymore.

Taulan and Iraluq came to tell us about it. They said
it was very quiet in the qasgiq for a few minutes after
Panruk did that. But then everyone began to talk and
eat as if nothing had happened. Taulan and Iraluq had
sparkling eyes when they told us. I didn't think they
liked Qanrilaq much, either.

When I heard what Panruk had done I almost
laughed with pleasure. I didn't know what Qanrilaq
had done, because Panruk would never complain to
me, even if we were like sisters all our lives. But I

could see that Grandma was glad as well, so Panruk must have told her something.

Panruk didn't say anything about it for days, but one night when we were lying on the benches, almost asleep, she whispered to me, "Qanrilaq said he would not let any girl babies live."

"Oh," I said. It was the custom to kill girl babies if times were hard, or if more children were not wanted, and it was up to the father to decide which children would live. Our grandfather had kept all of his girls.

"I don't want anyone to kill my girls," said Panruk.

When Mr. Hoff heard that Panruk had thrown Qanrilaq away, he came to our house to speak to Grandma and Panruk. We were sewing in the middle of the floor under the smoke-hole window, where the light was best. We'd spread a big seal skin out on the floor to keep our sewing clean.

Grandma kept her eyes on her sewing while Mr. Hoff explained why he was there.

Then Grandma said, "In the Yup'ik way, we think it is foolish to be with someone you can't get along with or who doesn't suit."

"But it is contrary to the law of God," said Mr. Hoff.

Grandma acted as if she hadn't heard. "I had another husband before Panruk's grandfather. After I learned what he was like, I didn't like him at all," she said. "I threw him away."

Mr. Hoff's mouth was set in a stubborn line. He was so cheerful and easy-going at home when we children were visiting that it was hard to believe he was the same person.

"This is a heathen practice," he said. "I must speak up because discarding a husband jeopardizes Panruk's chance to spend eternity in heaven."

I could see that Mr. Hoff really cared about what happened to Panruk, and I felt sorry for him. But I didn't understand why he thought going to heaven was so important if he didn't really know what it was like there. Maybe it wasn't nearly as nice as he thought, and when he got there he'd wish he could go somewhere else. I wanted to do something for him to pay him back for caring about us, so I got up and brought him the tray with dried fish and seal oil.

He shook his head no, and I saw Grandma's mouth tighten a little. It was very rude for a guest to refuse food.

"Is there any reason why she dislikes him? Perhaps he was abusive to her?" Mr. Hoff asked insistently.

Grandma lifted her head from her sewing and looked at Mr. Hoff. "In the Yup'ik way we don't interfere between a man and a woman. It is a private matter," she said calmly.

Mr. Hoff left then, and Grandma said nothing more about it.

I knew that Mr. Hoff had spoken out in the men's house about killing babies. Maybe if he knew why Panruk didn't like Qanrilaq, he would be glad she'd thrown him away. But probably not. With Mr. Hoff there weren't any in-between ways. It was all or nothing.

Mr. Hoff had had trouble getting people to listen to him in the summer when everyone was so busy, but after the snow came, he asked once a week to speak to everyone in the men's house.

I don't think anyone wanted to listen to Mr. Hoff, but it was the Yup'ik belief that everyone had a right to speak and that it was courteous to listen. One of the men would pound on the floor of the men's house with a big mallet. The women in their houses could hear that sound and would know that they were being called to the men's house.

Not long after he had come to speak to Grandma, Mr. Hoff asked to speak again in the men's house. He talked for a while about why we should join his religion, and when he was finished, Nusailak got up to speak.

Nusailak, who was the oldest man in the village, talked about the terrible smallpox epidemic that came with the Russians when he was a little boy. More than half the people along the Kuskokwim and the Yukon rivers died during that epidemic.

Nusailak and his friend had traveled down the river during the sickness and found many spring camps where every single person had died. The sod houses were full of people, all dead. All he and his friend could do for them was to collapse the roofs of the houses and shovel the sod over them. Nusailak said that the white people brought illness and that he didn't want these missionaries, or any of their ways, here. Maybe their religion was good for the white men, but it was not good for the Eskimos.

Mr. Hoff stood up quickly. "Stone axes were good enough for the Eskimos long before the Russians came, but now you use steel axes. No one would go back to the old ways and use a stone ax." He paused and looked around to see if anyone would disagree with that. "The superstitions of the shaman and the Yup'ik way of life are stone axes, and the way of life I offer you is a steel ax in place of stone." Mr. Hoff looked very pleased with himself when he finished speaking.

Then Grandfather spoke. He said he was very worried about sickness, like Nusailak was. He didn't think much of Mr. Hoff's religion, but he did like the white man's medicine. He believed that it would give the Yup'ik people more power over illness than the shamans had. He didn't think the missionaries had any power over the animal spirits, however. Just the shamans did. So, Grandfather said, perhaps the Yup'ik could have a use for both kinds of beliefs—Mr. Hoff's for power over sickness, and the shamans' for luck in hunting and fishing.

Before Grandpa got much further with that idea, Mr. Hoff jumped up again and said, "No, that's not possible. You must give up your shamans and your heathen superstitions."

My father was holding himself tightly, and although he spoke very quietly and calmly, I knew he was angry. He said that the white men could take their steel axes for all he cared, because since they'd come, we Yup'ik had had sickness, famine, bad fish runs, poor hunting, and few berries. "The animal spirits don't like the white man," my father said. "We know that because when we first used the white man's guns to hunt caribou, we killed many, many caribou, but the next year the caribou did not come back. Now," he said, "we have to go far away to find any caribou at all."

All around the qasgiq, men nodded their heads in agreement with what my father said.

"And haven't we all seen the Eskimos at Bethel, Eskimos who wear blue army coats with brass buttons instead of good parkas, and who do no work? They hang around the store and mission waiting for someone to give them something. Those men no longer follow any of the old ways," my father said quietly. "That's what white men have brought us—changes that take manhood away from Eskimo men."

There was a long silence in the qasgiq, and then Grandfather shook his head slowly. "Once changes come, you can't unchange them," he said. "Some of the things the white men have brought are good: matches, tea, knives." He stopped and smiled. "Tobacco—no one could do without tobacco." He was quiet again. "Boats," he said suddenly. "Wooden boats—birch-bark canoes and skin boats take a long time to make and tear easily on the rocks. The long saws the white men have make good boards, and wooden boats that don't tear on rocks can be made easily from those boards. So," said Grandpa, "we have taken some good things from the white people. Perhaps there may be other things they can give us that will help us all."

Cakayak's father spoke up to ask why the Yup'ik people needed Mr. Hoff's religion when the Russian priests had already baptized many in the old days.

"Oh, yes," said Mr. Hoff in an unpleasant way. "The Russians baptized you, all right. But they didn't teach you to be civilized. They didn't try to teach you how to change your lives. They just told you how to cross yourselves and take the sacraments."

Everyone felt ashamed for Mr. Hoff because he spoke without respect about the Russian priests. People liked the Russian priests because they had long robes and shiny crosses—and because they didn't try to change our ways.

Then Mr. Hoff told us what he didn't like about Yup'ik life. He thought that living off the land was bad because of lean years when fish and game were scarce. He thought the Yup'ik should earn a living by herding animals that didn't have to be hunted, and perhaps by digging in the ground for coal, which could be sold to the steamboats.

Mr. Hoff said husbands and wives should not separate from each other, ever, and that orphans should be treated as kindly as other children. Girl babies should not be killed. Men should not live away from their families in the men's house but should live with their wives and families, the way Mr. Hoff did.

Nusailak got up again. "If the men didn't live together," he said, "they might work just for themselves and their families, instead of for everyone. They might teach just their own children. When the men are together, we talk every day about what is needed, and who needs it. Each child has the benefit of all our wisdom, not just the wisdom of his or her own father. We work together to raise our children." Nusailak thought that living in just a one-family house would make people selfish, and being selfish is the worst thing a Yup'ik could be.

Mr. Hoff spoke again. Most of all, he didn't like the shamans, and he said that anyone who called on them for help was calling on the devil, the one who was in charge of hell and who was very bad. Mr. Hoff said that the shamans were tricksters who took things from people. "You can't really believe that the shaman goes to the moon, as he tells you," said Mr. Hoff loudly. He always grew most excited when he talked about the shamans. "The shaman only pretends to go to the moon—it is just a trick. He doesn't go to the moon at all. Such a thing is not possible."

Grandpa ignored what Mr. Hoff said about the shaman going to the moon and tried to explain to Mr. Hoff what the shaman's job was—how he smoothed the pathway for the animals to come to us. It was an important job, and one that a missionary could not do because he had no relationship with the animals.

The people in the men's house listened to Mr. Hoff with courtesy. When they asked questions or for explanations, they did so with great politeness, just as they listened to my grandfather when he said he thought there might be something to be gained from the missionaries, and just as they listened to my father when he said that all the changes were bad.

Mr. Hoff was not so courteous. He sometimes became very bad-tempered.

I felt more like my grandfather did than like my father. I thought about the exciting things I'd learned—writing and reading and all the things in the magazines. I was glad to have learned about these things, and glad to have things like beautiful calico and sugar. I didn't want to unlearn anything, or do without the white men's things we'd grown used to having.

But I liked our old ways, too. And I didn't like the idea of hell.

14 Miss Oakes

Poor Mrs. Hoff was very tired by the time winter came.

She had to supervise the washing of clothes and do the ironing, since no one else would do it. She had to see that David hauled enough water and did the schoolwork she gave him every day. See that her helpers cleaned the house the right way. Sew. Write letter after letter to the missions. Order supplies. Supervise the work the boys did around the school, like washing the stacks of dishes after every meal. Teach singing to the boys. Most tiring of all, she had to do all the cooking and baking for ten boys and her family.

In the wintertime Yup'ik women seldom cooked. We had frozen fish and dried fish, and seal oil and frozen berries. Once in a while, Grandma would boil fish eggs into a soup, or if one of our men caught a rabbit or ptarmigan, she might boil that in the big iron pot, but usually we ate our food frozen or dried, only twice a day. It didn't take very much time to fix meals.

Mrs. Hoff, on the other hand, was cooking all the time. She made three big meals a day for her family and for the boys at the school. Some of the boys liked kass'aq food, especially bread and hotcakes with jam, but none of them liked cooked mush. When I spooned the mush into their bowls in the morning, they rolled their eyes at me to show me how horrible they thought it was. I tried some and it *was* horrible.

Mrs. Hoff gave the boys Eskimo food, too, but instead of giving it to them raw or frozen, she cooked it first, because the Hoffs never ate uncooked food. Sometimes

they ate dried fish, but not very often. I wasn't sure
if they thought raw or frozen fish was heathen, but
anyway, they never ate it that way.

Mrs. Hoff never cooked anything whole—with the
guts still inside—and she didn't save the blood for soup.
She cleaned everything, removing all the feathers and
heads and feet and fins and skin. So cooking in the
Hoffs' way took a lot of time.

Just before the ice closed the river, the mission boat
came with three new people: a teacher, a nurse, and
Helper Jack.

Mr. Hoff brought them to the house and introduced
them to all the women who were working in the big
room. "I have to begin making trips to the other villages,
now that we've got the school built," he said. "I can't
do that and teach the boys, too, so Miss Oakes will
continue the work I've begun."

Miss Oakes was very heavy and tall—taller than
Mr. Hoff.

I couldn't see what color her eyes were because they
were scrunched up into smiling little fat rolls above
her cheeks, but her hair was almost the color of the

salmonberries, and it grew in little springy coils all over her head. I thought she couldn't be wearing a corset because her waist stuck out with rolls of fat, like handles, and it looked very soft.

The nurse was Miss Danfort. She had been working at the mission in Bethel, so she knew a little Yup'ik. Because our village was in the middle, people from upriver and downriver would now be able to come to her easily when they were sick.

She wasn't thin or fat, and her eyes and skin and hair seemed almost without color. There were deep lines around her eyes and mouth, and when she bent her head to the lamp, you could see that there was a lot of white in her hair.

"*Kass'angyarr,*" Cakayak's grandma whispered in an amazed way. "An old white person."

Miss Danfort already had good winter clothes that she'd had made in Bethel, but Miss Oakes had nothing but the clothes she'd brought with her from her home. So right away Mrs. Hoff set Grandma and the other women to sewing winter clothes for Miss Oakes. It took more than forty-five skins to make Miss Oakes a muskrat parka, and she had such big feet that Grandma and the other women complained among themselves that the boots they made for her were ugly.

Miss Oakes was to live in the little room off the schoolroom. I helped her paint the room. While we painted, I tried out my English on her. I had never spoken English to anyone but David before, and I was afraid the English words would fall out of my head when I needed them. But they didn't. They popped right in when I spoke.

And although sometimes she frowned and squinched her eyes together and looked puzzled, if I repeated what I'd said, her face always smoothed out and she would say, "Oh, of course!"

Miss Oakes was just like Mrs. Hoff—she wanted to make her room beautiful with pictures and cloth that hung on the wall and covered the bed and windows.

It wasn't very long before Miss Oakes was doing some of the cooking. She had a lot of energy and

Mrs. Hoff was so often tired. Miss Oakes made a lot of different things, especially sweet things. She made little pancakes rolled into a tube, and cookies, and rice cooked with milk and sugar into a pudding like akutaq.

The first time she cooked, the boys came back to her in the kitchen and said, *"Keniyuvagcit!* How well you cook!"

I told her what they had said, and you never saw anyone smile like Miss Oakes. She learned right away what *assirpagta* meant, too: "How good it is."

She liked cooking for the boys.

15 Helper Jack

Helper Jack was a nice young man dressed in the Eskimo way. He was very clean and neat, and he had very short hair.

After staying in our village for a few days, he was going to go on to Kulkaromute to work with the people there. Mr. Hoff thought Kulkaromute was a place where people were very eager to learn about his religion, and he couldn't be in two places at once.

Helper Jack had learned to read and write at Mr. Hoff's Bethel school, and every day he read the Bible to himself. The young men of our village were very interested in him, and he visited them every day in the men's house. Taulan and Iraluq liked to talk to him. They asked him why he had given up the Yup'ik ways to take on the new ways.

Helper Jack said that he could no longer believe that shamans did what they said they did. He thought, as Mr. Hoff did, that they used trickery to make people believe they'd been on the moon or had gone to the villages of the animal souls. They just did that to make people afraid, he said.

Taulan and Iraluq laughed and asked if he didn't think that hell was a story to make people afraid, as well.

They argued back and forth like that all the time that Helper Jack was with them. Taulan and Iraluq liked arguing a lot.

Then Helper Jack went by dog team to Kulkaromute, and we didn't know when we'd see him again.

Miss Danfort had a room next to Miss Oakes', which was to be used as a clinic. She had a little bed in there but nothing to make the room look pretty, the way Mrs. Hoff and Miss Oakes did. All kass'aq women were not the same, I could see.

I went to visit Miss Danfort in her room while she was putting away the medicine she'd brought with her. I had so many questions to ask her, but the first thing that popped out was, "Corset?" I pointed to her waist to show that I wanted to know if she was wearing one. I was immediately sorry I'd said that, because I knew talking about corsets made Mrs. Hoff fidgety. It was as Grandpa was always telling me. I should hold my lips together tightly while I thought about the thing that I was meaning to say.

"No," Miss Danfort said, not even looking surprised. "I don't wear them. And I never will. It's not good for your health, having your organs pushed around like that. No wonder women have fainting spells and need smelling salts!" She spoke so quickly, I couldn't understand her at all.

"Speak slowly, please," I said.

She said it more slowly and a lot louder then. I didn't understand organs or fainting spells, so she had to explain those words to me, but when she finally made me understand, I could tell that Miss Danfort was like Grandma and had opinions.

And like me, she didn't always agree with what everyone around her thought. I liked her very much.

"How did you learn to speak English?" she asked, with a little space between each word.

"I listen," I said. "And David helps me."

"You must learn languages very easily," she said. "I'm not half as good in Yup'ik as you are in English."

"English words are short," I said.

She laughed. "Well, certainly shorter than Yup'ik words. Yup'ik words are very long."

Mr. Hoff came into the room while we were talking and asked Miss Danfort if there was anything that she needed for her room. She told him how surprised she was that I spoke English.

"Yup'ik children are taught when they're very young to concentrate," he said. "They're expected to remember everything they hear, and they're expected to tell it back perfectly. I wish I'd been trained like that early in my life."

Miss Danfort looked at me intently. "I wish I had, too," she said.

"Besides that," said Mr. Hoff, "I think Minuk is an extraordinarily bright girl."

"I think you're right," said Miss Danfort.

I didn't know what that meant. When I asked David later, and he told me that it meant *smart*, I was very proud.

Miss Danfort had brought with her a *stereoscope*. You put a card of pictures called *stereographs* into the stereoscope and then you held it up to your eye. When you looked in a stereoscope, the pictures looked real, as if you could touch them, as if you could walk right into them. They weren't flat like the pictures in magazines or the photographs the Hoffs had.

Nothing the Hoffs had—not the magazines or the Kodak or the stove or the sewing machine—had caused that much excitement. All the women in the village came to look at the stereographs, crowding into the living room and talking excitedly until it was their turn. Only one person could look at a time.

A lot of the men came, even the oldest ones who

seldom left the men's house to go anywhere. Even
Nusailak. Of course my father and his friends didn't
come.

There were stereographs of circuses and zoo animals,
and historical buildings, and the Centennial Exposition,
and dozens of other things. I looked at them all, but
the one that I looked at over and over showed a big
flood called the Johnstown Flood, which had happened
just a year ago. It was so horrible. There were hundreds
of people left behind by the floodwaters, their bodies
flung about like driftwood.

Nusailak must have looked at the stereographs of
the zoo animals a hundred times. There was a picture
of an elephant being washed with a big broom by his
keeper. Nusailak went back to that picture again and
again. *"Angvaa, angvaa!"* old Nusailak kept murmuring
to himself. "How big, how big!"

Mr. Hoff told him that the elephant was the relative
of the big animals that the Yup'ik thought lived under
the ground, because we saw the bones only when they
washed out of the riverbanks. Mr. Hoff explained that
the bones were from mastodons and mammoths,

ancient elephants that had really lived long ago in our country but had died out. He said that those ancient animals were like first cousins to the elephant.

Nusailak just couldn't believe his eyes.

Miss Oakes was getting along fine in the classroom. The boys spoke enough English by now to understand her simple commands, and, although she couldn't speak Yup'ik, David translated for her when Mrs. Hoff was too busy.

I think the boys liked Miss Oakes's teaching better than Mr. Hoff's. Mr. Hoff was very kind most of the time, but Miss Oakes was very jolly, and she laughed a lot more than he did. The boys laughed when she tried to speak Yup'ik and she laughed at the way they spoke English, so there was a lot of laughing. And she never used the strap.

At home Mamma was making new clothes for me to wear at the winter celebrations. My pants were made of caribou legs, with strips of darker fur alternating with the lighter, to make a lovely striped pattern. I could hardly wait until it was time to wear them. My parka was of caribou with traditional triangles of the white belly fur of the caribou set into the shoulders, but Mamma had added something different to my parka. She liked to try different patterns and designs.

A long rectangle of golden muskrat-belly fur went down the middle of the parka between the triangles. Those two warm colors, the muskrat and the caribou, were beautiful together, just like the layers in the sky when the sun is setting. Tassels of wolverine tails hung about the back and shoulders of the parka, tassels that would move and sway with me when we did our dances at the festivals. Mamma made a beautiful ruff of gray wolf fur tipped with black, which would stand out in a perfect circle around my face. Inside the wolf fur she set a band of dark wolverine fur, which didn't frost in the cold air. The cuffs of the parka sleeves were trimmed with wolverine fur, too.

My parka showed what a good hunter my father was, able to give his daughter wolf and wolverine for her ruff. I could tell he was very pleased when

Mamma showed him how it was coming along.

"Look," said Mamma, showing him the fine work Grandma had done on the parka. All around the curved band of the bottom of the parka, Grandma had sewn in white caribou-belly strips with the hair scraped off, and around those strips were dark bands of tanned eel skin outlining the white. "People will know what a fine hunter her father is, when they see the beautiful furs in this parka," said Mamma.

My father almost smiled. "They will also praise the fine sewing her mother has done, which brought such beautiful furs to the hunter."

He said this because of the Yup'ik belief that animals come to the hunter whose wife sews well. The animals want to be used by a skillful sewer, not by one who will bungle the sewing and do a bad job with their skins.

My father was so often stern with Mamma and with all of us that I was glad that he'd said that to praise her. If I were a husband, I would praise my wife all the time, like Grandpa, and not just once in a while, like my father.

16 *A Time for Drumming*

In the Yup'ik language the darkest part of winter was called *Cauyarvik,* "a time for drumming." That's because we held our most important festivals then, and during a festival there was always dancing and singing to the drums. Sometimes the whole village would go to Kalskag or Avaucharak for a big weeklong festival. There were little festivals and dances, too.

People were very busy during the months before Cauyarvik, making new clothes and dance costumes, practicing dances and songs, and preparing the food and gifts that would be given away at festivals. We were so busy that few of us could help Mrs. Hoff as much as she wanted, and she complained to Mr. Hoff about the unreliability of villagers.

Sometimes people prepared their gifts for years.

When we gave a feast for Panruk's father, who died in the river when we were little girls, Grandma made twenty-seven pairs of fish-skin boots with woven-grass socks, twenty fish-skin bags, twenty-one fish-skin coats with a fish-skin bag for each, twenty-three grass baskets, and twenty-one grass fish bags, all to give away in remembrance of her dead son-in-law. And the others in our family made just as many gifts.

Mr. Hoff spoke about this custom in the qasgiq. When he was in Bethel, he had been dismayed by how many things were given away and how much food was distributed at Yup'ik celebrations. He hoped we were not so foolish in our village. He said that our big feasts wasted food and that it was wrong not to save as much food as possible for the hungry times in the spring.

He knew some people who had given everything they had to others, until they had nothing left. Those people were content because they'd shown so much generosity when they should have taken pride instead in saving. He said he thought that giving things away was not a good custom, but a foolish one.

The old men told Mr. Hoff that he must understand

that in the Yup'ik way, the more you gave, the more would come back. Just as when you were hunting: the more animals you killed, the more you would get the next year. Giving and sharing were an important part of Yup'ik life—maybe the most important part.

The Mask Dance was held every year during Cauyarvik. We children loved this festival best because the masks and animal carvings were so wonderful. The shaman was in charge of the Mask Dance because he was the only one who could speak to the animals in the spirit world and ask them to come back to us, so there would be a good supply of fish and animals.

It was the Yup'ik belief that the animals and people were equal partners in the universe, and that people must treat all animals with the greatest respect. In return, the animals would respect our needs and would provide themselves to us for food. Just as we believed that people were reborn into new babies, we also believed that animals were reborn, and if they had been treated respectfully, they would allow themselves to be caught again.

But we should have known that Mr. Hoff hated

shamans so much that there would be trouble.

For the Mask Dance we all dressed in our best clothes. Grandpa wore his labrets, ivory buttons that fitted into the holes pierced at each corner of his mouth. None of the young men had those holes. They weren't fashionable anymore, but I thought labrets made the old men look very dressed up. Iraluq and Taulan wore their short dance parkas and fancy long gloves and the new tall dance boots Grandma had made for them. They looked very handsome.

Mamma looked beautiful with her long beaded earrings swinging against her cheeks and her new parka ruff standing in rays around her face. Her hair was neatly braided and bound with beads, and two blue beads hung on sinew threads from the holes in her nasal septum.

I wore my caribou-teeth belt. It had belonged to my grandma's mother and was passed to Grandma, the oldest daughter, and then to my mother, also the oldest daughter, and finally to me. And I would give it to my oldest girl one day. There were hundreds of teeth on it. Many of the other girls had such belts, but I thought mine was the most beautiful.

I was so proud of everyone because our family was so beautifully dressed. I could tell that Mamma and Grandma and the aunts were proud, too.

After the men went into the qasgiq, Mr. Hoff asked all the women to stand in front of the men's house while he took pictures of us with his Kodak. Cakayak's new baby brother looked so funny, peeking out of his mother's parka, with his amazed face and his spiky black hair sticking up every which way, that we couldn't keep from laughing. I wished I had a baby brother like that.

We were laughing so hard that it took Mr. Hoff five exposures to get a picture when no one was moving. He said he would print the photographs later and show us how we looked all dressed up. I could hardly wait to see those pictures.

The animal carvings were hung all around the center of the men's house, where they could watch the dances the men did for them. These were beautifully made, one for each kind of animal and fish. The special masks the men wore while they danced and sang for the animals were just as wonderfully carved.

Panruk and I sat watching and holding our breath. We knew these were not real animals, but the dances the men did showed so perfectly how each animal moved, and the calls the men made to imitate the animals and birds were so real, it was as if we were really in the spirit world of the animals.

Mr. Hoff had never seen the Mask Dance, so he and David had come to watch. David came to sit with Panruk and me. David liked the dances as well as we did, I think, because he was holding his breath, too.

Everyone had to be absolutely quiet while the dance of each animal was being performed, because it was believed that the spirits of the animals were in the qasgiq and that they would take fright if there was too much noise.

But in the middle of the ceremony, Mr. Hoff suddenly

jumped to his feet, and he shouted at the shaman.
He said the shaman was the devil's helper and that
this festival was the worst kind of heathenism. Like
everyone else, David and Panruk and I sat frozen in
our places.

Then the men stood up and quietly told Mr. Hoff
to leave. My father and Kanlak went to Mr. Hoff and
took him by the arms and led him out of the qasgiq.
David gave us a frightened look, and then he got to
his feet and followed his father.

The shaman and the men still in the qasgiq began
to make loud squawking and cawing noises. Panruk
and I didn't know why they were doing that, but
Grandpa told us later that it was to convince the spirits
of the animals that the noise they'd heard was that of
ravens. The men were afraid that the animals' spirits
might take fright and leave after Mr. Hoff's shouts
because they were offended at being treated so disre-
spectfully. Then perhaps they would not listen when
the shaman asked them to come back to us.

The people were already upset that Mr. Hoff had
tried to interfere with Panruk and Qanrilaq, and that

he had not understood the giving and sharing at our festivals. But his interference in the Mask Dance was far worse. He had perhaps ruined the hunting and fishing for the year with his loud interruption.

The people in the qasgiq sat quietly, heads down, after the cawing and squawking stopped. Then Nusailak stood and gestured to the dancers to continue, but the joy had gone out of the ceremony. Everyone was frightened and sick at heart. This time Mr. Hoff had gone too far.

Later, Mr. Hoff tried to speak to the men again, but when he came into the men's house, everyone got up and left. They would no longer accept his presence in the men's house.

I was sorry for Mr. Hoff with his kind brown eyes, because he wanted so much to help us. But he was so loud and rude that no one would listen to him anymore.

A few days after the Mask Dance, Grandpa and I went out to sit on the bank to watch the northern

lights. In the Yup'ik legend, the northern lights were
spirits of dead boys playing ball, and when the lights
shifted back and forth, quick and jerky, that was the
boy who caught the ball, stumbled, and then threw it
across the sky again. Some nights the lights were deep,
dark colors. Grandpa had seen them twice when they
were blood red, and all the snow around was red from
the reflected color. That was supposed to predict a
terrible battle, in which the ground would be covered
with blood. I would have liked very much to see a red
aurora, but not if it meant so much trouble. Grandma
had told me that she had seen them one night with all
the colors of the rainbow, but most nights they were
pale, pale green and pale pink or white.

Grandpa showed me a cluster of seven little stars.
They were called the Little Foxes. The three stars
close together in a row were called the Great Stretcher,
he said, because that was where a giant length of rawhide rope was being stretched and dried.

Then Grandpa got to his feet and brushed the snow
off his pants. "Come," he said. "We'll go to Grandma's
house. I want to talk to you women."

Grandma boiled water and made some Labrador tea. I think she knew what Grandpa was going to say because she kept trying to get him to eat something, and she kept trying to talk about things that might interest him and make him forget why he'd come.

Grandpa finished his tea and put the bowl aside. Then he looked at us very seriously. "The men have decided this," Grandpa said. "We will not allow our women to work for the Hoffs anymore. I think it's good to learn new ways, though not all the men agree about that. But Mr. Hoff has abused our hospitality by interfering with the Mask Dance. We didn't ask him to come here, and we won't be interfered with anymore." He said that Kasruq, the orphan, was leaving the school and coming back to the qasgiq.

Panruk and Grandma and I looked at the floor. I knew Grandma was fond of Mrs. Hoff, in the way an old woman is fond of a young woman who is sometimes foolish. She liked coming home and amazing Mamma and the aunts with another story of something strange Mrs. Hoff had done.

And I would miss going to the Hoffs' very much.

I would miss David, and jolly Miss Oakes, and joking with the boys in the morning when I dished out their oatmeal. I'd miss the magazines and the catalogs, and the stereoscope and the mirror. I'd miss my dress with the white apron and the pocket, and I'd miss the soap.

Maybe we wouldn't ever get to see the photographs Mr. Hoff had taken of all of us women before the Mask Dance, when we were all laughing and dressed in our best clothes.

I would miss talking to Miss Danfort and learning her opinions. And oh, I would be so sorry not to know what the boys were learning. I was just a little way into the first reader, and now how would I ever be able to finish, or go on to the second? Perhaps I'd even forget how to speak English.

Why did Mr. Hoff have to do that? Why couldn't he have held his tongue, as Yup'ik people do? Why did he have to have such bad manners?

17 Miss Danfort

A few days after Nusailak told Mr. Hoff that the village women could not work for him or his wife, Miss Danfort sent David to the men's house with a message for my grandfather: Would he please let her speak to him about something very important?

Grandpa went at once to the clinic, for he was very courteous and wouldn't make her wait. Afterward, he went to the qasgiq to tell the men what Miss Danfort had asked, and then he came to our house.

"The nurse wants Minuk to work for her," he said. "She says Minuk can speak and understand enough English to help her, and she is sure that Minuk's English will get better rapidly because she learns so fast." Grandpa continued, "Miss Danfort says that her job is to cure diseases, not to civilize people or

change their beliefs. She is a member of the Hoffs'
church, but she is not doing church business in her
clinic. She wants our people to become more healthy."

My breath nearly stopped in my throat. We all
waited to hear what else Grandpa would say. "The
white men have good medicine. We know they can
cure many things which would not have been cured
in the old days by the shaman, and that is the truth,"
he said. "Yup'ik women can become shamans, so it's
not against our customs for Minuk to work for the
nurse and learn what she knows. She can help our
people." Grandpa stopped talking and looked at me
very seriously. Then he said, "The men in the qasgiq
have agreed that Minuk may work for the nurse."

I put my head down to show my acceptance, but

I wanted very much to cry and laugh and shout at the same time. I was so pleased that Miss Danfort had asked for me, and I was so very pleased that I'd be learning something new, and speaking English, and peeking in the schoolroom to learn enough to finish book one.

Miss Danfort had a big thick book called *The United States Dispensatory*, which listed all the medicines and what they were used for. I wished that I could read it.

People came from every village along the river to see her, so we often had someone staying with us in Grandma's house. Often there were men staying in the qasgiq who had come to see the nurse. Some people thought that she knew more than the shaman.

Mrs. Hoff was still very angry about what had happened in the qasgiq, when all the men had walked out when Mr. Hoff tried to speak.

"We shouldn't let anyone come to the clinic who isn't a member of our church," she snapped. Mr. Hoff and Miss Danfort looked at her so strangely that

Mrs. Hoff patted her hair in the back and said, "Well, maybe not."

>✈

Miss Danfort had brought with her a big box of eyeglasses, which had been given to her church for the missions. I had a wonderful time looking through those glasses. Some of them made everything look completely smudged, some made things look far away, and some were in-between. Mr. Hoff wore eyeglasses to read with, and so did Miss Oakes, but no one in the village had ever had eyeglasses.

Pretty soon all the old people were wearing eye-glasses, and they were very pleased that they could see well enough again to sew or do the fine carving they used to do before their eyes got bad.

Maklak thought eyeglasses were the most interest-ing things he'd ever seen and he wanted a pair badly. He went to see Miss Danfort and told her in great seriousness that he couldn't see anything anymore and that he needed glasses. I was so embarrassed.

"Miss Danfort," I said, "there's nothing wrong with Maklak's eyes! He's just pretending so he can have eyeglasses."

Miss Danfort just laughed. "I don't think he'll be wearing them long," she said.

Maklak wore them for a whole day, proud as anything. He peered at everybody like some funny kind of owl, until he found that the metal wires hurt the backs of his ears, the glasses slipped down his little nose, and the nose pieces pinched. He brought them back to Miss Danfort and told her that he could see again.

"You really have to need glasses to ignore the discomfort they cause you," Miss Danfort told me.

When I heard that, I was glad my eyes were good.

Grandma had a blue film growing over her eyes, which made it hard for her to see in the bright sunlight. Miss Danfort said it was a *cataract* and that a doctor could take it off. She said she would send Grandma in the summer to the doctor at the Nulato hospital up along the Yukon River. Grandma smiled and nodded when I told her in Yup'ik what Miss Danfort had said, but I knew that when the summer came, Grandma would never go all that way to the hospital. She had never been even to Bethel, which was much closer.

When someone came to see her, Miss Danfort always listened to the sound his chest made when she tapped on it with two fingers. She said she could tell that way if someone had tuberculosis. A lot of people did, but she said that they probably wouldn't get any worse because they spent so much time outdoors. Most of the cases she'd seen in Bethel got better.

"Listen," she'd say to me. "Do you hear that thick sound his chest makes when I thump it?" I smiled and nodded, but I didn't hear. All the chests sounded the same to me, so I knew I wouldn't be a very good nurse.

A lot of people came with toothaches. Miss Danfort had a pair of forceps she used to grab the bad tooth, and then she'd tip and twist the tooth until it came out. I helped her pull out those teeth, but I hated it, because the teeth made such a horrible sucking sound while they were being pulled. It must have hurt terribly, because the people who were having teeth taken out pulled so hard on the armrests of the chair that the arms got wobbly and Mr. Hoff had to nail them down again every few days. But even the children were very brave and didn't cry out. I didn't think I could stand it if I had to have a tooth pulled out.

"I thought about being a dentist," Miss Danfort told me. "But now I'm glad I didn't do it. It takes a lot of strength to pull teeth!"

"Can a woman be a dentist?" I asked.

"Yes, there are a few," she said. "Actually, I really wanted to be a doctor, but when I was a girl, they didn't allow women into the medical schools."

I thought about what she'd said for a minute. "Why are there so many things that they don't want girls to do?" I asked.

Miss Danfort looked at me and made a rude sort of sound. "Why, indeed?" she said.

One day Miss Danfort sewed up the scalp of a man who had cut his head badly. I had to talk and talk to explain to him why his hair had to be shaved off first, but finally he could see that it would be hard to sew up such a wound without getting long strands of hair in it. There was blood everywhere. I had never seen so much at once. Miss Danfort said not to worry, that scalps always bled like that, but so much blood made my knees shake.

She helped Teksik deliver her new baby, because the baby was turned around backwards and wouldn't come out. Miss Danfort turned the baby around with long pincer-like things and the baby came out fine, with the little blue mark at the base of her spine that all Eskimo babies have. She was so pretty. I was glad that Mr. Hoff had raised such a big fuss about letting baby girls live. I was pretty sure that Teksik and her husband would keep her.

Then the shaman from Kalskag accidentally shot himself with his gun, and he asked to be brought to Miss Danfort.

He said the shaman in another village had caused the accident to happen with his spells and magic. When I translated this into English for Miss Danfort, she gave him a cold, hard look and said, "What nonsense." Miss Danfort, I could see, didn't like shamans any better than Mr. Hoff did.

The shaman had taken a charge of shot through his left arm and shoulder. It had broken the bone and left a hole filled with splinters of bone and shreds of cloth. Miss Danfort cleaned the wound with boiled water and antiseptic, and with tweezers took out all the splinters of bone and shreds of cloth. Then she put the ends of the bone together. I didn't watch what she was doing while I boiled bandages and handed her what she needed, because my stomach was feeling queasy.

When she was finished, she gave the shaman some laudanum to help him sleep. He slept in the clinic for two whole days, and then he moved to the men's house to stay until his arm healed.

Mr. and Mrs. Hoff were happier than I'd ever seen them when the shaman came to their clinic. "He can't pretend anymore to have power, if he can't heal himself," Mr. Hoff said. "I think this is the end of shamanism."

And there must have been some truth in what Mr. Hoff said, because even old Nusailak came to the clinic the next week to have a boil lanced.

18 *Mellgar*

One lovely bright afternoon, when the trees were
thickly frosted and beautiful against the blue sky, a
messenger came to Mr. Hoff from Kulkaromute. Miss
Danfort and I watched out the window of the clinic as
Mr. Hoff went out to greet the man. We knew it was a
very serious message because the man didn't take his
dogs out of harness or put his sled away before he came
to see Mr. Hoff.

We saw Mr. Hoff bow his head and cover his face
with his hands, and we knew something terrible had
happened. The man handed Mr. Hoff a fish-skin bag
and then got on his sled and drove his team toward the
men's house. Mr. Hoff brought the bag into the house
and set it on the floor by the door.

Mrs. Hoff came out of the kitchen, wiping her hands

on her apron. As soon as she saw his face, she said, "My dear, what is it?"

"You must prepare yourself for bad news," he said.

Miss Oakes came to the door of the classroom when she heard the tone of his voice, and soon the boys were crowded around her in the doorway, looking with solemn faces at Mr. Hoff.

"Helper Jack has been killed by the people of Kulkaromute," he said. Mr. Hoff had to stop talking until he could get his voice under control. We all just stood and stared at him while he rubbed his face.

I was so sorry, because Helper Jack had been such a nice young man.

After Helper Jack was killed, the people of Kulkaromute had gathered everything in the village that had come from the mission—tea bags, Helper Jack's Bible, needles and pins, and a little hat Mrs. Hoff had made for one of the babies. Every single thing that belonged to the mission and Helper Jack was put into a fish-skin bag and the bag was put onto the sled. The men of the village told the messenger to bring everything back to the Hoffs. The messenger said the people didn't want anything to do with the mission anymore, because mission people interfered in the Yup'ik way.

The grown-ups began to talk so fast and excitedly that I could hardly understand their English. I could tell, though, that Mr. and Mrs. Hoff blamed the shaman of Kulkaromute for Helper Jack's death.

Miss Danfort sent me home so she could comfort the Hoffs, and Miss Oakes told the boys to go to their room upstairs. When I went out the door, I saw that the grown-ups were all on their knees in the big front room, praying.

>≫

One cold night, Grandma and Mamma and the aunts and Panruk and I were sewing around the oil lamp when Grandma spoke suddenly. "Minuk, Nusailak's grandson, Mellgar, has asked for you."

They didn't look at me—they just waited to see what I'd say.

I didn't say anything, so Grandma said, "If you like Mellgar, his aunt will begin sewing for you."

I just kept sewing and still didn't say anything, but I was thinking very hard. When I became a woman, Mellgar would be my husband. Imagine that. He'd hunt for us, and I'd take care of the meat he brought home. I'd take food to him in the men's house, and help him with his sled and dogs, and one day we would have children together. I'd see to it that his clothes were patched and that he had new ones when the old ones wore out. I would be a good woman, and he would be proud of me.

Mellgar was not like Panruk's husband. Mellgar laughed all the time. Even when his face was still and he was serious, listening to the old men, his eyes looked to me like they were laughing. And when the young men played their games on the river, Mellgar was one of the liveliest ones, and he never got mad when he lost a race or a contest.

I looked at Maklak, and I could see he was having a hard time not saying anything, because he was biting his lip and looking at me out of the corners of his eyes. Mellgar was Maklak's favorite in the men's house because Mellgar paid attention to him. When Maklak

threw snowballs at him, Mellgar threw them back and
then chased Maklak and pretended he would throw
him in the water hole. Mellgar and Maklak were a lot
alike, I thought. Mellgar remembered what it was like
to be a little boy. I was sure he wouldn't kill our first
baby if she were a girl.

So I looked at them. "Yes," I said.

You should have seen Maklak's smile.

The days grew longer again, and it was time to go
to spring camp again.

While everyone was getting everything ready to
go, two Yup'ik men came across the portage from their
village along the Yukon River. They were going to the
trading post at Kolmakov. After they'd been welcomed
in the qasgiq and given something to eat, the village
men asked for the news from the Yukon.

Grandpa came to our house later and told us everything the visitors had said. There were many white
people on the Yukon River now, they said, and they

had brought a lot of trading goods with them. They wanted wood to fuel their steamboats, so many people along the Yukon were cutting wood for them. There were steamboats going up and down the river all summer, and they had seen a barge with horses going to the mining claims.

I would have loved to see those horses.

One of the men said there had been a lot of sickness along the lower Yukon, terrible coughs and fevers that made people see things and talk out of their heads. Many people had died.

I told Miss Danfort what the men said.

"I heard about that epidemic," she said. "They had diphtheria and whooping cough and chicken pox last year, but now it's influenza, which is very bad. Very bad indeed."

"Do you have medicine for that?" I asked her.

"There isn't any medicine for influenza."

"Did you ever see anyone with influenza?"

"Yes," she said. "Many times. First patients feel sick and ache all over. They have high fevers and bad coughs. Then their lungs are affected, and they can't breathe anymore. They can die very quickly." She looked very worried. "I pray that it won't come here."

>≫

Mellgar's family left for their spring camp after the Yukon men went on to Kolmakov. I was glad of that because when Mellgar was in the village, I was always trying to look at him without looking, and Grandma and the aunts teased me that my head was not where it should be. But he was very nice to look at, and I was proud that he was going to be my husband. Once Mellgar turned from his dogsled while I was passing by and smiled at me, one of his small, secret smiles, with his eyes crinkled up.

Someday we would be like Grandma and Grandpa, sitting on the bench together, quiet like good friends. And someday he would praise me for being a good woman.

Cakayak's mother became very ill after Mellgar's family left, and in a few days she died of influenza. Miss Danfort thought the Yukon men had brought the sickness because Cakayak's mother had been the one who had brought them food and mended their boots.

Her body was carried to the men's house and put on a bench in a sitting position, with her knees folded up and tied with thongs. Her head was down, as if she were thinking of something.

The women and children came into the men's house and began to grieve for Cakayak's mother, rocking back and forth, howling and crying out, "*Arenqiapaa! Arenqiapaa!* How terrible!"

It *was* terrible, and Panruk and Maklak and I clung together and cried, each of us thinking how it would be if it were our mother.

No one in the village could work that day or use any sharp knives or axes. This was because Cakayak's mother's soul would be in the village for one day, and it would be angry if it cut itself on the sharp things. Also, the name soul would be coming on the trail to inhabit the body of a new baby, and it was important not to cut the trail of a name soul.

The next day, her husband and brother-in-law built

a square box of planks, which they decorated with beautiful designs. One of the men carved the face of a woman on a spruce pole that would be set in front of the grave box. He used Grandpa's dye box to paint the hair and eyes.

When everything was ready, the body of Cakayak's mother was lifted through the smoke hole of the men's house. Her husband put her into the square box and fitted the lid, and then the men in her family carried it to the graveyard, with all of us following.

The grave box was set on four poles and the carved stick was set into the ground in front of it. Her favorite things—her tin teakettle and sewing kit—were set on the poles so they could go with her to her new life.

I was sorry for Cakayak, who stood in the snow with her little brother strapped on her back. What if it had been my beautiful mamma?

Maybe I would be the first one to have a new baby, and if I did, I would name it Atsaq, for Cakayak's mother.

The next day, Grandpa and Father and Uncle Aparuk and Taulan and Iraluq packed the sled with

everything we'd need for spring camp. It was
unusually cold for that time of year, but the trail was
hard, so we would have easy going. Our two dogs
were so happy to be put in harness that they barked
and lunged on their lines. It had been a while since
they'd been on a long run.

When we were all ready to go, I ran to say good-
bye to Miss Danfort and to everyone at the Hoffs'.
They said they hoped we would have a good trail and
that the hunting would be good. Miss Danfort took
me aside and gave me a copy of the first book of
McGuffey's Reader.

"Here," she said, and winked at me. "I kidnapped
this from the schoolroom." That meant she had taken
it without asking. "You can practice while you're gone."

I had thought no one knew about my reading, but
all along Miss Danfort knew. And she thought it was
all right! I smiled at her. But I couldn't take the book.
"Miss Danfort," I whispered. "No. My father will be
angry."

Miss Danfort looked at me for a minute and then
she nodded. "Certainly," she said. "I understand.

You'll be back in a short time, and you can start again. I won't worry about you forgetting your English words—not with your memory. And when you get back, I'll help you."

19 *Sickness*

Our camp was so deep in snow that we almost
couldn't see the house, just the cache standing tall
on its four legs. Taulan and Iraluq took the wooden
shovels and threw themselves into clearing the snow
from the front of the house, and soon they had cut a
neat, deep trail through the clean layers of snow to
the passageway of the house.

Then we brought most of the bundles from the
sled into the house and stored the rest in the cache.
Grandma lit the moss in the stone lamp, and there
we were, at camp once again.

It was always so good to get back to camp and be
just by ourselves. Even my father seemed happy as we
sat by the fire after our first dinner, and he told a long,
long story about Raven and the sunlight.

But Mamma began to cough that night when everyone was asleep, and she called to me to bring her water. She said she hurt all over. Of course we had been a long time on the trail, and perhaps she ached from hard walking in deep snow. And a cough was an ordinary thing. Many people got a cough from time to time. It wasn't anything to worry about.

But she wasn't better in the morning, and although Grandma covered her with the big muskrat blanket, Mamma said she was cold.

Grandpa made a fire in the house when she said that, but Mamma's cough became tight and painful, and her face was red with fever. It wasn't long before she didn't know us, and she cried out and talked wildly in her sleep.

Grandpa had wanted me to work for Miss Danfort
so I would learn things that could help our people. But
I had learned only that nothing could be done about
this illness. I was so ashamed to disappoint him. I sat
by his side on the bench and held his hand and we
watched together.

Mamma thrashed around so much that she was in
danger of falling off the bench, so we put her caribou
robes on the floor and laid her on them. Grandma and
the aunts and Panruk did everything they could to
make her comfortable. They took her earrings out so
she wouldn't tear the holes in her ears, and they dipped
feathers in water to wet her mouth, but she died
anyway, her hair all tangled and matted with sweat.

When she stopped breathing, Grandpa went outside
and looked for boards to make a grave box for Mamma.

My brother Iraluq began to weep and looked just
like a little boy again, crying, "Mamma, Mamma."

Maklak was like me, stony still.

The next day Grandpa got sick, and then Iraluq
and Auntie Naya. They lay on their caribou robes and
sweated and cried out and begged for water, more water.

They coughed and choked, and when I thumped their chests with two fingers I heard nothing. But when I put my ear to their chests, as Miss Danfort had taught me to do, I heard the crackling noise of ragged breathing.

Auntie Naya died in a few days, but Grandpa and Iraluq lived longer, seeing such terrible things, and crying out in such horror, that I was glad when they fell silent.

Taulan pulled them out of the house by the feet and put their bodies under the sled rack. By then Auntie Nanagak and Auntie Kakgar had begun to cough, and then Maklak began. One by one, the others got sick and died: Grandma and our father and the aunties, and then Taulan as well. Only Uncle Aparuk, Maklak, Panruk, and I were still alive.

And then our quiet uncle got sick. He was so noisy and so talkative in his fever that we hardly recognized him. Laughing and staring wildly at the wall, he told one story after another from his childhood. They were stories we'd never heard. Why couldn't he have talked like this before?

Uncle Aparuk and Maklak were so thin that their

skin seemed shriveled on their faces and arms. Panruk
and I went from one to the other, spooning fish broth
down their throats, trying to keep them warm, trying
to get water down them, and wiping their faces, which
ran with sweat when the fever was the worst.

Then Panruk got sick, and I took care of her, too.
She was almost better when I began to cough and felt
pain in my bones that seemed impossible to bear. None
of our family had told us how badly they hurt, how
even their skin ached, but now I knew why some of
them had died so quickly. It was because they hurt so
badly that they wanted to die. They wanted to go and
be finished with the pain.

Then I didn't know anything more at all.

When I came to myself, Maklak was taking care
of me. He'd gotten better, I could see that from his
eyes and skin. The house was quiet, except for the
crackle of wood in the firepit. Who was cooking?
Panruk? I lifted myself up to look around the room.

There was Uncle Aparuk, on the bench by the door.

"Where's Panruk?" I asked Maklak.

Maklak didn't look at me.

It was impossible to believe that quiet, quiet room. No one singing or talking or working, there were no stories, no sounds of sewing or cooking or carving or eating. No sounds of illness or fever or soothing voices giving water. Just the popping of the fire.

"Just you and me and Uncle Aparuk left?" I asked. Maklak shook his head.

"Uncle Aparuk is dead," he said. "I couldn't move him out of the house."

According to our beliefs, the dead could not stay in the house with the living, so we had to move him.

Maklak was weak and I was exhausted. My legs shook so badly, I could hardly stand. But together we pulled Uncle Aparuk's body out and under the sled rack with the others. Then we covered them all with the big sealskin tarp.

I tried to remember their faces, but I could see nothing, just the mound under the sled rack. Nothing at all. I couldn't remember them, I couldn't build grave boxes for them, and I couldn't even flex their knees and put them in the proper position. I couldn't keep the shrews from them. I didn't know what would happen to their spirits or their name souls if I didn't do things right. And I was too tired to think of what I had to do. I couldn't even keep on my feet anymore, and I sank down into the snow. Maklak pulled at my arms roughly.

"Minuk, get up! You must get up!"

I don't know how long I knelt there in the snow, but finally I got to my feet. I leaned on Maklak's thin shoulders, and slowly we got back into the house. I fell onto the bench and slept. I slept for a long time again, maybe days, and woke only when Maklak made me drink water and spooned fish broth into my mouth. He wiped my face the way he'd seen Panruk and me do for the others.

"I didn't know you could cook," I said to him the first time he woke me with broth.

"I didn't know, either," he said.

When I fell back to sleep, he tried to keep me awake. "Tell me a story, Minuk," he begged. "It's so quiet when you're sleeping."

"Yes," I said. "I'll tell you the story of the woman who married a bear." But my eyes wouldn't stay open and it was too much work to speak.

Finally one morning, I awoke and felt stronger. My eyes were clear and I could see across the room. Little Maklak was by my bench, sleeping on the floor, his body rolled in a ball, the way he'd slept when he was a baby. He'd brought both dogs in the house, and they looked at me and thumped their tails on the floor when I sat up. Grandma's lamp was burning on her bench, and clothes and tools were scattered all over. The pot Maklak had been cooking in was crusted with grease.

"I've got to get up," I said. "I've got to clean things up."

Maklak sat up suddenly when I spoke, and he looked into my face. "Stay awake, Minuk. Please stay awake," he said.

"Yes," I said. "I'll stay awake. I'm better now. Did

you bring the dogs in to keep you company?"

"Yes," he said. "It was too lonesome in here."

I held out my hand to our white dog, and he came to the bench and pushed his nose against my cheek. "You took good care of me, Maklak."

I could see that Maklak was not the same little boy, because praise didn't make him look proud.

"Maklak," I said. "I'm so hungry. Will you get me something to eat?"

He brought me a wooden bowl of dried fish he'd cut into little pieces, and he put seal oil in it. I ate it all and asked for more. His little worried face smoothed out when he saw me eating.

"Could you boil me some water for tea?" I asked.

He went outside with the wooden bucket and brought it back full of snow to fill the kettle. I got off the bench slowly and tried walking. My legs were not too shaky as I squatted by the fire and blew on it to make the flames go higher. Blowing was very hard. I didn't seem to have any air in my lungs.

There was a pile of wood by the firepit. Maklak had brought wood in to keep the fire going. I looked at him with gratitude. He'd kept the fire going to make broth, he'd chopped the fish into little pieces, he'd brought seal oil from the cache, and he'd kept the lamp burning. And we'd thought he was just a baby.

We made the tea, and Maklak brought me one of the little packages of sugar Mrs. Hoff had given us for picking berries. That tea tasted wonderful and I drank two bowlfuls. Then I was tired again.

But I couldn't rest until I'd cleaned up. I stripped my clothes off and washed all over, even my hair. Maklak had spilled fish broth all down the front of my parka while he was feeding me, so I took Mamma's old parka to wear instead.

"Maklak," I said, "I'm still weak, but I'm much better. I'm going to sleep just a little while this time."

"Yes," he said, but his face was worried again.

Every day I grew stronger and stronger. I cleaned up the house and folded the scattered clothing. I scrubbed the pot with sand and put away Grandma's sewing.

But all the time, my throat ached as I thought about our family out there under the sled rack. If I didn't do what was right for them, perhaps I'd never be able to see their faces or the way they walked, or hear the way they sounded. Perhaps that was why I'd lost their memory. I was the one who was left behind. It was my responsibility to see that things were done correctly.

"Maklak," I said, "you and I must go to Mellgar's camp and get their help with the boxes. As soon as I'm strong enough."

"Yes," he said. "Mellgar will help us." I could see that the thought of Mellgar made Maklak feel better.

It made me feel better, too.

So when the day came that I was well enough, we put on our heaviest winter clothes and put the harnesses on the dogs. We put enough food for two days into a bag in case we got lost, and I got a bag of blackfish from the cache for the dogs. I put Maklak in the sled and wouldn't let him run along with me because I was so afraid that he'd get sick again.

We drove away with our eyes straight ahead, not turning our heads to look at the mound under the sled rack. Then, at the last minute we both turned to look, as if we couldn't help it. And I could see them, suddenly, just the way they'd looked the time I went with Cakayak's family to the festival at Kalskag, when I was young.

They'd all been standing in front of the ena, and Grandma was waving. Maklak was little, his head peeking out of Mamma's parka, and Mamma and the aunties had their arms around each other. The boys were laughing and shoving each other, the way they always did. My father and Uncle Aparuk were quiet, smoking their pipes, arms folded, just watching us, and Grandpa, oh Grandpa, had that look on his face, that sweet, kind look he always wore. And there was my Panruk, in the front, smiling good-bye. I could see them all so clearly, just as they had been that day.

I felt such a stab of terrible pain that I put my foot on the brake to stop the sled, and I bent over the handle-bars, unable to move for a minute. The dogs turned and looked at me, but Maklak kept his eyes straight ahead and shook the sled with an impatient jerk.

"Let's go, Minuk! Let's go!" His voice sounded so strange, I wondered if he'd seen them, too.

We traveled all day, over the trail that was blown free of deep snow and so was easy going, for it was still cold. Maklak had seen to it that the dogs had eaten well while everyone was sick, so they had no trouble pulling the sled and Maklak. I tired so easily that we stopped often. We had to stop so much, I didn't think we'd get there in one day.

But late in the evening, when the full moon was high overhead, we reached Mellgar's camp. We saw no smoke coming from the house and no people moving about. I bent low to go through the passageway into the house and I heard nothing, not a sound.

I knew what I'd see.

In the bright moonlight streaming through the smoke hole, I could see them all lying dead on the benches and on the floor. There, by the door, was Mellgar. And there was his auntie, the one who had been making my marriage clothes, and old Nusailak. Old Nusailak and his elephants.

With both Nusailak and Grandpa gone, I thought, the men's house would not be the same. They were the two old men who spoke all the time, always trying to work things out.

I climbed on top of the house and I knocked in the

poles that held the roof, the way Nusailak had told us he had done long ago, during the smallpox epidemic. The sod around the poles and the grass and the snow fell down on top of all the people in the house, while tears ran down my face and froze my eyelashes.

Maklak was so sorry that his friend Mellgar was gone that he stayed in the sled with his head down and didn't look at what I was doing.

"We must go back to camp and bury our family, too," I said, "for there's no one to help us with the boxes."

Maklak began to cry. "No, not back to camp. Let's go home," he said.

As soon as he said that, I knew it was a good idea. "Yes," I said. "We'll send someone back to take care of them."

We spent the night in the cache, and by morning the cold weather had broken. We fed our dogs and took some of the fish from the cache, and we began to go toward our village.

By late afternoon it began to snow thickly. The wet, heavy snow made a lot of overflow on the creeks and created places where the water oozed up from cracks in the ice. We had to be careful not to get wet, or we would freeze our feet. We took our time crossing the creeks and lakes and didn't take any chances. I walked in front of the dogs to break the trail for them because the snow was so deep. We went very slowly, because we were so tired. And because there was no hurry.

There was no moon and no stars because the sky was heavy with clouds, and snow came down every day. Soon every branch and twig was coated with heavy wet snow.

At night I made a snow house—the way Grandpa had shown us—and when we put Grandma's oil lamp inside, we were as warm as could be.

We traveled only part of the day because we didn't really want to get back to the village. We didn't want to begin life in our house without our family, we didn't want to see the men's house without Grandpa and Nusailak, and without our father and Uncle Aparuk and Iraluq and Taulan and Mellgar.

While we struggled through the deep snow, we didn't have to think about the things that had happened, and we didn't have to look at all the ways our lives would be different.

20 Going On

We could see the lights in the Hoffs' house and in the school when we came around the bend in the river. Maklak and I stopped and stared at the school. We couldn't seem to decide what to do next, now that we'd reached our village.

The village dogs were barking at our dogs, and in a few minutes Teksik came out of her ena. She gave a little scream when she saw us. She stroked Maklak's face and laughed a little—and cried, too.

"Where are the others?" she asked.

"Dead," said Maklak.

"Nusailak's family, as well," I said.

Teksik's husband and some other men came from the qasgiq and took our sled and dogs away while Teksik took us into her ena. She gave us fish and boiled water for tea while we told her what had happened.

Teksik was so happy that I didn't die, so that her little girl could still be alive to her. The glad way she looked reminded me of the way Mamma smiled sometimes, and that made me cry. My tears felt so hot streaming over my cold face, as if I were bleeding or as if hot water were pouring down my cheeks.

Maklak fell asleep before he'd had anything to eat. He must have been very, very tired.

Teksik said that shortly after we left the village, the influenza epidemic struck before most of the people had left for their camps. Most of them had died. Everyone thought that maybe Mellgar's family and ours had escaped it because we'd left the village early.

All the babies in our village were gone, every one. Even Cakayak's baby brother with the spikey hair. And Teksik's new baby girl. And many, many of the old people. Two of the boys in the school had died, and Miss Danfort had been very sick herself.

Kasruq, our village orphan, was still alive. He came to Teksik's ena to say that he and Teksik's husband would go to our camp to bury our family.

I knew that Kasruq was the one who would ask for me now. When he came back from our camp, he said nothing about what he found there, but he brought me my mother's clothes and all the other things I'd put in bags. He looked at me sympathetically to show me that he was sorry for my loss. I knew he had lost everyone, as well, long before Maklak and I had.

The spring leaves were out and the water in the river was running free of ice before Miss Danfort was on her feet again.

The soldiers at St. Michael were sent along the river to make coffins and bury the dead. In all the eight villages above us, only sixty people were left alive. Below us it was much the same.

No one had been able to hunt or fish during the epidemic, so the soldiers brought food to all the survivors: pilot bread, corned beef, bacon and beans, canned milk, sugar, and tea. So we ate nothing but white people's food all spring.

The Hoffs were getting ready to move to another village closer to the mouth of the river. They had not been successful in our part of the country, and, after Helper Jack's death, they had no heart to keep trying. They also wanted to go to a bigger place, since our village was so small now that so many had died during the epidemic.

But they hadn't known whether they should stay or go, so Mrs. Hoff said that Mr. Hoff had stood the Bible up on its spine and then let it fall over and open by itself. He said that wherever the book opened, there would be a message from their god telling them what they should do. And the book had opened to a place that said, "a King of Assyria turned back, and stayed not there in the land," so they decided that meant that they should leave our village.

That was sort of like the way the shaman would see what the spirits wanted us to do by looking at the insides of a fish. The Hoffs would have said that was a heathen superstition, though.

Mr. Hoff gave us a copy of the picture he had taken of all the village women the night of the Mask Dance.

We could hardly bear to look at it, with all the laughing happy faces that now were gone. But we were so glad to have it.

Three of the boys at school had shown themselves to be very likely helpers, so they were going with the Hoffs. The rest would go back to their villages. Miss Oakes was going to the Bethel school to teach, and Miss Danfort was going to go back to Maryland to try to get her strength back.

"Minuk," she said to me one day, "I want you to come with me. You are very, very clever, and not only at learning languages. You learn everything very quickly. I think you should go to school. I'd like you to go to the school I went to. I'll pay for your schooling." She reached out and touched my face. "Perhaps you could become a nurse if you worked very hard. Maybe even a doctor."

I looked at Miss Danfort and smiled. Imagine, going to Maryland. I'd see the telephone and the bicycle and wear those high-buttoned shoes. Would I have to wear corsets in Maryland? There would be steamboats, and trains, and cows and pigs, and houses crowded with things. For just a minute it sounded wonderful to be in a place without sickness or sadness or memories or hunger.

Then I laughed and shook my head. "Miss Danfort," I said, "how could I do that?"

She looked at me sadly. "I thought that's what you'd say," she said.

"There's so much to do," I said.

All the girls and women who were left in the village had been very busy, sewing for those whose mothers or aunties or grandmas had died, and weaving the grass bags and mats and baskets we'd need for the summer's fishing. We had to put our heads together to try to remember how to do the things we needed to do. So much had been lost with our old people.

We all wished we had listened harder and learned more.

But how surprised we were to see that people who had been quiet and unassuming before the sickness began to step forward. Teksik's husband, who had said so little before, was often the one who would stand in the men's house and talk to us about what we must do.

"Didn't old Nusailak," he said, "tell us many times

about the smallpox epidemic long ago? That was a
time as terrible as this, and yet the ones who were
left had carried on and had, as ever, shown the Yup'ik
ways to the young. This is why Nusailak told us about
those times, so that we, too, could be strong when our
hard times came."

When he talked, I could just see Grandpa sitting
on the benches, nodding his head in agreement. I
could just feel how he'd smile and praise us and would
expect us never to be discouraged.

So, of course, I couldn't go to Maryland with
Miss Danfort.

I must stay here and be a good woman.

The End

Then and Now ♦ *A Girl's Life*

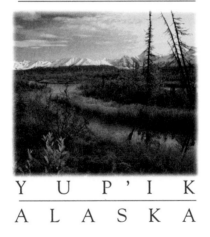

Y U P ' I K

A L A S K A

Minuk's people belonged to the Yup'ik Eskimo, who live in western Alaska and Siberia. The Yup'ik are part of the larger family of Eskimo cultures that stretches for thousands of miles across the far north, from Siberia to Greenland. Some Eskimo people lived along the arctic coast and hunted walrus and seal from kayaks, but others—like Minuk's people—settled along inland rivers, where life was very different.

Minuk's story takes place in 1890, in the *taiga* (*tie-geh*), or forested country, along the upper Kuskokwim River of western Alaska. For most of the year, the Yup'ik in this area lived in villages of sod houses dug partway into the earth. They were skilled at using all the plants and animals available to them through the changing seasons, but they depended most on the salmon and other fish in the Kuskokwim.

In this part of Alaska, summer temperatures average about 60 degrees, and winter temperatures drop to −50 degrees and colder. In this climate, good clothing could mean the difference between life and death. The knowledge and skill needed to produce the specialized clothing of the Yup'ik passed from mother to daughter for generations.

Everyone in Minuk's village—men, women, and children—dressed much the same way. In the warmer months, they wore lightweight, loose-fitting parkas of caribou hide. Winter clothing was heavier and warmer. Minuk's winter parka was made from the pelts of arctic ground squirrels, and the hood was trimmed with wolverine fur, prized because it does not frost up when exposed to

All Eskimo clothing was made of fur, skin, or hide, but the specific material depended on both season and location.

A waterproof parka of fish skin or dried seal intestines could be worn in rainy weather.

warm breath. Under her winter parka, Minuk wore fur trousers tucked into caribou-skin boots. During winter's bitter cold, people often wore two parkas and two pairs of trousers. They frequently wore the inner layer with the fur next to their skin, while the outer layer was worn fur-side out. The air trapped between the two layers was an extra insulator.

Women made all the clothing. Yup'ik women were so skilled that they could make their stitches nearly invisible, sew delicate material like dried fish skin as well as tough hides and furs, and make clothes that fit perfectly without using a pattern. They took pride in decorating clothing with contrasting fur insets and trims. Girls began learning to sew at an early age, but they were adults before they

Women stored their needles in delicately carved and decorated needle cases made of bird bone or ivory.

mastered the art. A girl's skill in sewing was her greatest asset in marriage, just as a boy's was his skill in hunting.

For hundreds of years, the Yup'ik along the Kuskokwim lived much the way Minuk's village did. Their lives changed with the seasons, and their traditions helped each village work together to survive.

In the late 1700s, European explorers reached the Alaskan coast, bringing diseases that were

If an Eskimo woman had a baby to carry, her parka could be made extra roomy in back, so the baby could nestle next to her warm skin.

deadly to the native people. Russian fur traders reached the Kuskokwim River in the 1830s, and the first smallpox epidemic hit there in 1838. Within a few months, more than half the Yup'ik along the Kuskokwim were dead.

As more Russian and then American traders and missionaries trickled into the region, waves of influenza,

Russian Orthodox missionaries built this frontier cathedral in Sitka, Alaska.

Native girls at a mission school

measles, and smallpox hit the native people, wiping out whole families and villages. In 1900, an epidemic of influenza and measles struck nearly every Kuskokwim Yup'ik and killed at least half.

By about 1910, the Kuskokwim Yup'ik had been reduced from 4,000 people to 500. Many villages were abandoned, and traditions were lost because few elders survived to pass them on. One missionary along the Kuskokwim wrote, "The population now consists of the younger generation—like the second growth of timber—with here and there a middle-aged person."

Missionaries brought other changes, urging the Yup'ik to abandon their traditional ways, become Christians, and adopt American education, medicine, dress, foods, manners, and ways of making a living. Some Yup'ik accepted Christianity or found ways to blend Christianity with traditional Yup'ik beliefs.

Eventually, the epidemics stopped, and the Yup'ik population began to grow again. Today, some Yup'ik children grow up in cities, but most still live in Yup'ik villages. They can buy frozen pizza at the store, go to school, and surf the Internet, but they also hunt and fish, speak Yup'ik, and listen to legends that have been told for generations. From their elders, they learn traditional arts, such as dancing and making fur clothing. Yup'ik people today are not only surviving, but working hard to keep their traditions alive in a changing world.

Yup'ik girls today

Glossary of Yup'ik Words

Yup'ik has its own sound system, which is hard to reproduce in English, so these pronunciations are only approximate.

agu *(AH-goo)*—"Don't!"

akutaq *(AH-koo-tahk)*—a mixture of berries and fat

angvaa *(AHNG-vah)*—"How big!"

arenqiapaa *(ah-REN-kee-pah)*—"How terrible!"

assiipaa *(ah-SEE-pah)*—"How awful."

assirpagta *(ah-sihr-PAHG-tah)*—"How good it is."

Cauyarvik *(chah-YAHR-vik)*—the darkest part of winter; it means "the time for drumming," because many festivals with dancing and drumming take place at that time

ena *(nah)*—a women's house

kass'angyarr *(kass-AHN-gyahr)*—an old white person

kass'aq *(GUSS-uk)*—a white person; derived from the Russian word "cossack"

keniyuvagcit *(kehn-ee-YOO-vahg-sit)*—"How well you cook!"

qasgiq *(KASS-gik)*—the men's house

qaspeq *(GUSS-puk)*—a parka cover made of cloth

uluaq *(OO-loo-ak)*—a woman's curved knife

Yup'ik *(youp-ik)*—a native Eskimo people of south-western Alaska

Pronunciation of Yup'ik characters' names:

Aparuk *(AH-puh-ruk)*—Minuk and Panruk's uncle

Atsaq *(AT-sak)*—a village woman, Cakayak's mother

Cakayak *(KAK-ee-yak)*—a village girl, a friend of Minuk's

Iraluq *(EAR-uh-luk)*—Minuk's older brother

Kakgar *(KAK-gahr)*—Minuk's aunt and Panruk's mother

Kanlak *(KAN-lak)*—a village man

Kasruq *(KASS-ruk)*—a village boy who is an orphan

Maklak *(MAK-lak)*—Minuk's younger brother

Mellgar *(MEHL-gahr)*—a village boy

Minuk *(MIN-uk)*—a twelve-year-old Yup'ik girl

Naya *(NAY-yuh)*—Minuk and Panruk's aunt

Nunagak *(NOON-ah-gak)*—Minuk and Panruk's aunt

Nusailak *(NOO-sahl-ak)*—the oldest man in the village

Panruk *(PAN-ruk)*—Minuk's cousin and best friend

Qanrilaq *(KAN-rih-lak)*—Panruk's husband
Taulan *(TAU-lahn)*—Minuk's cousin
Teksik *(TEK-sick)*—a village woman
Uliggaq *(OO-lih-gak)*—a village girl, a friend of
  Minuk's

Pronunciation of place names:
Avaucharak *(ah-VOW-chahr-ek)*—an historic village
  along the Kuskokwim River
Kalskag *(KAHL-skag)*—a town along the Kuskokwim
  River
Kolmakov *(KOHL-mah-kov)*—an historic village
  along the Kuskokwim River
Kulkaromute *(kool-KAHR-oh-myoot)*—an historic
  village along the Kuskokwim River
Kuskokwim *(KUS-ko-kwim)*—a river in western
  Alaska
Nulato *(noo-LAH-toe)*—a town along the Yukon
  River

Author's Note

As a child who liked history, I sometimes found Alaska to be a very frustrating place to grow up, because everything was so new. The oldest house in our town was only forty years old.

Of course, the Indians and Eskimos had been in Alaska for thousands of years, but there was no written record, and anthropologists had to speculate about what their lives had been like before the Europeans came. And those early people left little behind them of that old life but artifacts, whereas I wanted to tour stone castles, walk on the Great Wall of China, and stand in the circle at Stonehenge.

But the good thing about growing up in Alaska was that it was possible to talk to people who had been there *almost* at the time of the first contact with Europeans. Along the Yukon River, where I spent much of my life, the first Russians came in 1845, and many of the old people remembered what their parents had to say about that first contact.

When my stepfather's mother told me the stories of her mother, who remembered the first white man she'd ever seen, I was fascinated. I tried to imagine what it must have been like to first see mirrors, cloth, and writing, and to taste sugar and bread.

So her stories were the beginning of my interest in the process of *acculturation*—what happens when one culture comes smack up against another culture. This has been happening from the beginning of time: the Cro-Magnon meet the Neanderthal, the Syrians meet the Egyptians. And it has happened in Australia and Africa and the South Pacific, and everywhere else.

Because I'd thought and read and heard so much about these first years of contact in Alaska, Minuk's story almost wrote itself. Although Minuk is a fictional character, the things that happened in the story—sometimes very sad things—were taken straight from the journals and documents of the time.

Kirkpatrick Hill